DOUBLE CHALLENGE!

Breck Malone looked up. Two men stood there, men with holsters tied low to their legs, men who carried the arrogant assurance of their gun speed. One was fair, one was dark, but they walked with the same panther stride, they both wore the same half-grin.

Gunslingers, Breck thought, and he rose, hand dropping smoothly down near his holster. Only a flick of their eyes disclosed that the two men had seen the movement. They halted a few feet away.

The dark one spoke. "You the gent who shot Red Hollings?"

Breck kept his voice level. "I am. And you look like you need some of the same."

Lee E. Wells
TARNISHED STAR

AVON
PUBLISHERS OF BARD, CAMELOT, DISCUS, EQUINOX AND FLARE BOOKS

AVON BOOKS
A division of
The Hearst Corporation
959 Eighth Avenue
New York, New York 10019

ISBN: 0-380-00853-X

First Avon Printing, September, 1960
Fifth printing

Printed in the U.S.A.

Chapter I

FROM THIS DISTANCE, San Alma looked exactly as it had when he rode out ten years ago. Though still many miles away and dwarfed, it looked amazingly clear and the long, slanting rays of the setting sun, shining directly down the valley, made little pinpoint reflections of light on occasional windows. The twin steeples of the courthouse and the church lifted above the wide scattering of houses. The road out of the pass dropped down into the valley and undulated to the distant town.

Breck Malone cuffed back his hat brim and his eyes drank in the valley, bounded by the rock escarpments of the forbidding Thunder Range to the north and west and the Granada Mountains, through which he had just threaded, to the south and east. Looking at them, Breck wondered why he had been afraid they might change. They were as eternal as the washed blue bowl of sky, as the sun that always, late afternoons, sent soft shafts of golden benediction over the valley. These things did not pass away.

He did not check the horse as it ambled out of the pass and down the slope, but Breck's eyes drank in the rich, rolling grass, then lifted toward the Thunders. He smiled—long, crooked lips quirking in a pleasant way—when he recalled how he had asked Uncle Jim if outlaws hid up there.

The smile vanished. Uncle Jim Malone was dead now. Breck wished again that he might at least have been at the funeral. But the letter had chased him over half the southwest and the old man had been buried before Breck had started north.

He shook his thoughts loose and his gray eyes again looked down in the valley. The town had not grown so far as he could see, probably never would. He wondered if Jip Terry still ramrodded the law with his mild voice and swift, deadly gun. Jip would be getting old by now. Not so fast. Mellowed.

Breck sighed at the old memories and wondered at himself. He had given little thought to San Alma since he left, but now, coming back, he realized the place had been in the back of his mind all these years. Takes roaming, he thought, to appreciate what a man has left behind. But he was back, and maybe the old threads, with some changes, could be

5

picked up again. His long jaw set as he looked south and west beyond the town. Over there lay the ranch—his property now and, with it, an obligation to carry on and build up what Uncle Jim had started.

By the time he reached the outskirts of San Alma, the sun was behind the western peaks. The sky was still clear with touches of pink, but purple shadows crept slowly into the valley.

Breck straightened with new anticipation as the road became the main street. He rode tall and loose-jointed, angular face alight as he recognized house after house. Strangers might live there, but the buildings themselves were unchanged, out of the past.

He came into the few short blocks of the business district. Up ahead, the white, two-storied frame of the courthouse could be glimpsed through the greenery of the cottonwoods about it, only the spire rising sharp and clear. The hitchracks before it were empty now, the business of the law and the county being finished for the day.

There was Jan's Livery Stable. Up ahead, the protruding sign of the Bon Ton Store; the high, roofed porches of the Thunder and the Cattleman saloons; the stout permanence of the sheriff's office and jail; the Palace Hotel and Dane's General Store and Emporium.

Breck's chest expanded with a deep breath. Nothing changed—even the lines of saddle horses before the stores. He turned in toward the Thunder Saloon and dismounted.

Afoot, Breck still gave an impression of height and power—a big man with broad shoulders and narrow hips around which hung a cartridge belt, with a holstered gun on his right hip. He idly noticed the brands on the near horses at the rack as he beat the dust from his clothing.

His mouth pursed as he frowned. These were brands he had never seen in San Alma. There must be many more ranches, and he wondered how there could be enough room in the valley for them. He circled the rack and climbed the steps to the saloon porch.

As he approached the door, the batwings swung open and a man stepped out. He stopped short, black eyes in a stubbled face cutting at Breck with sharp, hard suspicion as his right hand jerked slightly toward his holster.

He sidled around Breck as if to keep him constantly in sight. He descended to the street and was gone. Breck half turned, frowning. This was a wrong note in the friendly town that he had known. He could have sworn the man wore the subtle stamp of the outlaw or gunman. Probably not, though. Jip wouldn't let that kind light for over five minutes.

6

Breck pushed through the batwings. At first glance, the big room was exactly as before. Not a fleck of dust seemed to have been moved from the rows of bottles behind the bar or a fly speck from the big mirror.

Then he realized that the talk and drinking had stopped. He became aware of sharp scrutiny from the men at the tables and at the bar. He didn't know any of them and again he felt the rise of hackles.

For a moment Breck had the feeling that this was not the Thunder Saloon but a gathering spot for renegades and hunted men. Then he saw the bartender and old memories rushed back. He forgot the men at the tables as he strode to the bar. The angles of his lean face softened and his gray eyes glowed as he thrust a long arm across the mahogany to the old man with the fringe of gray hair around a balding dome. "Tom Wheeler! You old goat! Remember me?"

Wheeler hitched at the cloth apron around his ample middle. He peered myopically at Breck a long moment and then recognition struck in a burst of light.

"Breck Malone! Man! It's been—how long?"

"Ten years."

Wheeler spun bottle and glass to the bar. "On the house, boy. Where have you been all that time?"

Now that the stranger had been at least partially identified, there was a renewal of talk at the tables and the men at the bar turned to their drinks. Breck could feel the easing off of tension as he grinned at Wheeler.

"Mostly down along the Arizona and New Mexico border," he answered. "Punching some, trail herding once or twice. Mostly riding the itch out of my heels. Foreman at a couple of places."

Wheeler leaned on the bar, peering at Breck. "Looks like it did you good. Filled out and growed up to fill your britches since you worked for the Circle M."

Breck chuckled. "I guess I gave you some trouble, Tom."

"Shucks! No more'n any hell-bubbling twenty-year-old would do. I knowed you'd grow out of it. I used to tell Jim Malone that when he'd get to worrying about you."

Breck's face fell. "Uncle Jim tried to make a top hand out of me."

"I'd say he done it, from the looks of you." Tom sighed. "I sure miss him. Only sixty, and I'd have sworn he'd live for another twenty years. You never know, I reckon."

He saw Breck's glass was empty and refilled it. Breck reached in his pocket for a coin and Tom bristled. "Your money ain't no good—at least this time. You spent enough in your day so that I ain't losing anything now."

Breck accepted with a nod and Tom again leaned his elbows on the bar. "So you're back, and mighty welcome. Hear Jim left you the spread. Heading out there?"

"Tonight."

"Aim to run it?"

"I reckon. Circle M's a good spread."

The old man's eyes went to the men at the end of the bar, then back to Breck. "Always figured that way," he said with a dryness Breck missed.

Breck looked about the big room. "Sure looks the same. Nothing changed in the town that I can see. But people will look a little older, I guess."

Tom pursed his lips and looked at the other men. "The town's not changed much—at least along the street. Same stores, same houses, and you'd see *them* first. But there's been changes. Other ways and more important."

Breck's brow arched. "How?"

"Well, now—" Tom started. Then he looked beyond Breck and hastily reached below the bar for the bottle. His voice became crisp. "Another one?"

Breck shook his head. He became aware of a movement behind him and a glance at the mirror showed two men just beyond his shoulder. He turned as one of them walked to the group at the far end of the bar. The other man faced Breck.

Breck noticed two things at first. The man's smile, though wide and flashing, just escaped warmth and friendliness. He wore a star on the left pocket of his gray wool shirt. He was tall, about Breck's age—one of those men whose fair skin is in startling contrast to dark eyes and coal-black hair. There was a lean competence about him from the easy set of the wide shoulders to the hand that rested lightly on his hip, not far from the gun nestled in the oiled-leather holster.

Breck took a second look at the badge and read the word "Sheriff," realizing with a shock that this was another of the changes in San Alma.

The man misread his thoughts. "That's right, the law." His voice was as easy as his stance, but Breck knew both could vanish in an instant.

"I expected Jip Terry," Breck said.

The man thumbed back his hat to reveal a widow's peak above the smoothly tanned forehead. "Jip? You must be an old timer . . . but I haven't seen you around before."

"Just come in. I'm Breck Malone."

"Jim Malone's nephew? Welcome back to San Alma. I'm Roy Cantro."

"Cantro?" Breck frowned slightly as he accepted the lawman's hand, felt the strength of his grip. "Cantro? Say, you're the one who cleaned up Tres Cruces, down in New Mexico."

Cantro's smile flashed wider, with real warmth now. He signaled Tom for drinks for himself and Breck, who tried to refuse. "Nonsense, Mr. Malone. It's the least I can do to welcome Jim's nephew. San Alma lost a fine, fine man when he died. Here's to his memory."

Breck could only accept the drink and the toast. Cantro replaced his glass. He shook his head. "Tres Cruces. That was years ago. My first law job."

"What brought you to San Alma?" Breck asked.

"Jip Terry was getting old and wanted a deputy. The pay was good so I took it. A year later, he resigned and I finished his term. The folks re-elected me and—well, I've been here almost eight years."

"A long time."

"I like the town and the people like me. I plan to stay as long as they'll keep me." He studied his empty glass. "Are you going to run the Circle M?"

"I don't know. I'll look it over first." Breck grinned. "I figured to be out there by now, but between you and Tom, there's been too many free drinks. I just wanted to look in and ride on."

"Glad you did. If there's anything I can do, Malone, sing out."

"Thanks."

Breck swung away from the bar and Cantro, flipping a coin on the counter, turned with him. He waved at one of the hard-eyed men at a table.

Breck pushed through the batwings, Cantro just behind him. As he crossed the porch, he noticed that the shadows had lengthened. It would be completely dark before he reached the Circle M. He cast a glance up and down the street, once more noting the familiar signs.

Cantro smiled. "Nice town. It's treated me good. I like it."

Breck nodded. Then his attention swung to the Cattleman Saloon, almost directly across the street. The batwings opened and a man half stumbled down the steps to the street. He caught his balance, stood swaying, then straightened and stared owlishly toward the Thunder. Breck recognized the same breed of man he had been encountering since he entered the town. Cantro watched lazily.

"Little too drunk, ain't he?" Breck asked.

"He'll sleep it off after a while," Cantro shrugged. "They take care of themselves."

Breck knew for certain that the law in San Alma had changed. The man started across the street, weaving slightly.

9

His lips were slack and moist. Coarse hair fell from beneath his hat into his eyes. He reached the near walk and then saw Cantro. He pulled up short and lifted his hand in drunken camaraderie. "H'llo, Roy. Have a drink?"

"Too early, Tex."

The drunk shook his head. "Never too early, Roy. You know that. You gonna howl, you gotta start soon's you can. Me, I'm howlin'."

He pulled his gun from the holster, pointed the muzzle to the sky and pulled the trigger. The blast made the horses at the racks skitter and snort. Two men by the barber shop wheeled about and discreetly moved into the building.

The lawman grinned wider as Tex holstered the gun and labored up the steps. "Really gonna howl, Roy," the drunk said.

"Get your drink and take it easy, Tex." Cantro half shoved the man toward the batwings. Before Tex could get control of his legs, he was within the saloon and Breck heard the lift of voices greeting him.

Breck shot a glance at the lawman. "A Colt and a drunk can be a mighty mean combination."

Cantro's smile thinned, then he laughed. "Tex means no harm. I'll pass word to his friends to take him home before he gets in trouble. No use cluttering up the jail."

"I guess not," Breck said dryly. The two men had reappeared before the barber shop and he wondered if this was a common incident. "I'll be getting along, Sheriff. Glad to know you."

"Good luck, Malone."

Breck descended the steps, mounted his horse and wheeled it into the street. Cantro lifted a hand in a friendly gesture. Breck answered and moved along, slowly.

What a change! he thought. If Jip Terry still wore the badge, that drunk would have been disarmed and arrested before he hit the street. He began to understand what Tom Wheeler had hinted at.

"Breck! Breck Malone!" A woman's voice lifted in surprised delight.

Breck jerked out of his thoughts and looked toward the walk. A woman looked eagerly at him, her lovely face lit by a warm smile.

Breck reined in, frowning. He did not know her, and yet, somewhere he had seen that long and delicate face with the high cheekbones, the chin with the shadow of a cleft. He removed his hat.

"Ma'am?"

Her eyes widened. They were blue-violet, set beneath

straight, thin brows. She wore no hat and her reddish-brown hair was combed back from a high forehead and done into a bun at the nape of the slender neck. Her full red lips parted as she looked at him in amazement and amused anger.

"Breck Malone! You of all people. Don't you know me? I'm Alice—Alice Dane."

His jaw dropped. He tumbled off the horse and stepped to her. She held out her hands and he grasped them, still staring at her face. The last time he had seen her she had been thin and gangling, all elbows, knees and moon-eyes as she watched him.

Now she was almost as tall as he. Her plain dress with the little lace collar about the neck could not conceal the feminine figure, the deep swell of the breasts, the narrow waist. The full, shoe-length skirt still suggested long and lovely legs.

He shook his head in amazement. "Alice, I'd never believe it! How you've changed."

"For the better?"

"A real woman!" He caught himself, and felt the flush on his cheeks.

She laughed. "Thank you, sir. At least you notice me. You never did before, except to get mad."

He stammered a faint excuse for past blindness and she laughed again. Then she sobered. "You've come back to take over Uncle Jim's spread?" He nodded. "I'm glad, Breck. Uncle Jim wanted that. He missed you more than you'll ever know. I wish he could see you now. He would have liked the kind of man you are."

Breck made a helpless gesture. "I should have stayed, but —well, fiddlefoot."

"Uncle Jim understood. He just hoped you'd come back sooner. But you, Breck. What have you been doing?"

He told her, scant words covering ten years of roaming. He grinned and shook his head when she asked if he were married, then shot the same question at her.

"No," she answered.

"The men in San Alma must have gone blind."

She looked impishly at him. "They always were. I remember one who rode off without looking twice." Before he could recover, she glanced over her shoulder at her father's store. "I have to get back. I saw you riding by and left a customer. Breck, as soon as you're settled, come out to the house. Dad would love to see you again."

"Just Dad?"

The color on her cheeks told him he had evened the score. "Thanks, Alice. I'll do that. Don't know when, though. It

11

might take a while to get hold of things at the ranch. But I'll come."

She smiled and turned to the store. He watched her until she disappeared and then, with an amazed shake of his head, swung into the saddle.

Behind him, Cantro still stood on the Thunder porch, a frown appearing. From where he stood, he hadn't been able to hear what was being said. But he had not missed the way Breck had looked at the girl, eyes traveling over her figure. He'd watched their animated gestures with no expression except narrowing eyes.

He thoughtfully passed his hand over his jaw. He could understand this renewal of old acquaintanceship, but he didn't like its warmth. He looked down the street a moment longer, then pushed open the batwings and disappeared.

Breck rode along with a bemused smile, hardly noticing that store fronts had given way to houses that grew more scattered as he neared the western end of Main Street. He saw, instead, Alice Dane as he had known her. Uncle Jim had traded at Dane's store and, every time Breck had gone there, Alice had contrived to wait on him, even if she had to abandon a customer.

He recalled how she had looked up at him from under long, dark lashes and how he had grown uncomfortable and stammering, half angry with the schoolgirl who could so upset a grown man. Breck recalled how Uncle Jim had gently teased him about his "sweetheart."

He chuckled. Look at her now! A man could be mighty proud to have a girl like *that* for his sweetheart.

He dismissed her as he passed the last house and the street changed into a dusty road that forked just ahead. He took the path to the left, thinking how many times he had passed this junction. The other fork led straight west for several miles to a pass through the Thunder Range.

Breck did not hurry. Despite the gathering shadows, the range was as familiar as the palm of his hand.

A star showed clear and bright despite the light streak in the western sky that gradually faded as shadows reached upward and engulfed it. A night bird cried a soft welcome. Far off to his right, he saw a gleam of light and he frowned, not being able to place it. Then, as the road dipped and the light was gone, he knew it was the Running W ranch house. His memory had slipped a notch in ten years.

As the last of daylight disappeared, a full moon rose over the eastern peaks and a silver light flooded the valley. Breck touched his horse with the spurs, realizing that he had best press on before Tip and whatever crew there was had gone to bed. Besides, for the first time, he was hungry.

The quickened pace covered the miles and he came to a narrow road that branched off to the left. He saw the faint dark shape of a sign. He pulled a match from his pocket and flicked it into flame with his fingernail as he bent down toward the solidly supported board.

Circle M—Jim Malone, he read in the crudely burned letters that he had sunk so deeply with a hot running iron.

The match snuffed out and he straightened, touched spurs to the horse and rode at a faster pace down the dim trail. The land was no more than a dark shadow, bounded to the south by the rugged Granada peaks that he could sense rather than see. But he knew each turn of the road, each lift and fall of the slopes over the rolling hills. He felt a rising excitement as the miles passed. Just beyond the next turn, the ranch itself would appear.

The swale between two low hummocks curved to the right and the moment he made the turn, he saw the distant gleam of light. He involuntarily reined in. Bright moonlight touched the buildings: the long and rambling ranch house, the squat oblong of combined bunkhouse and cookshack, the high peak of the barn roof, the tangle of corrals and pens.

His heart lifted and he suddenly wanted to hurry. He touched the horse into a pounding run. The whip of wind against his face added to his excitement, his eagerness to see Tip and to step inside the ranch house.

The buildings loomed higher and darker as he approached and he saw that the light came from a window in the bunkhouse. Then it went out and he could picture Tip and the crew rolling into their blankets.

He raced along the road, heading directly for the ranch house. Then he realized that he was acting like an excited kid and he slowed to a pace more suited to the owner of a ranch. A smile formed on his lips.

It vanished as gun flame blossomed near a corral and a bullet whined to his left. He shouted in alarm and pulled the horse to a sliding halt. A Colt roared from another direction and the slug whipped through the darkness—close, searching for him. A third shot whispered to the right.

Breck vaulted from the saddle and raced away from the snorting horse. He whipped his Colt from the holster. His eyes narrowed and he felt the pull of muscles as his jaw set and hardened.

Circle M had received him with bullets.

13

Chapter II

BRECK DROPPED FLAT. He would have been cut down except for the tricky moonlight that cast ink-black shadows but still revealed the slightest movement. A gun blasted again. Breck saw the spurt of orange flame beside the dark shape of a low bush.

He lifted his gun and his thumb dogged back the hammer. He heard a faint sound off to his left—ambushers starting a deadly circling movement. In a matter of minutes, he would be in a cross fire. His eyes narrowed and his lips flattened as he centered the gun muzzle on the distant bush. His finger tightened on the trigger, but some instinct checked him.

"Hold your guns!" he called. "I'm Breck Malone."

He flattened himself in case bullets searched toward the sound of his voice. The silence vibrated with tension. Breck chanced another slug. "Did you hear me? I'm Breck Malone!"

A startled oath sounded in the darkness and Breck thought he recognized the voice. Another voice sang out, "It's a trick, Tip."

"Tip!" Breck called. "What kind of welcome is this?"

The burred voice to his left called an order, tight and wary. "Hold your fire, boys. You, out there—come out slow and easy. Just remember you're flirting with a forty-four slug."

Breck holstered his gun and slowly stood up. His figure was outlined in moonlight and he felt moisture pop out on his palms.

"We see you," the harsh voice called. "Walk ahead and keep your hands high."

Breck lifted his arms and moved forward. He could not understand this reception and, though he was certain the voice was Tip's, he still took a long gamble and knew it.

He had taken only a few steps when the voice called again, very close now. Breck saw the outline of a low bush just ahead and to one side of the road. "You got a gun lined on you. Strike a match and show your face. Use your left hand —and nothing sudden."

Breck slowly lowered his hand. He fished a match from his shirt pocket and his nail flamed it just before and below his face, a target no one could miss at such close range.

The bright flame lit Breck's hard jaw, craggy brows and

14

high-ridged nose for an instant and then snuffed out. But it was enough. He heard the glad lift of the burring voice.

"By God, it is! Welcome home, boy!"

A shadow materialized into the shape of a short and stocky man. He strode forward, holstering his gun, and the moonlight revealed a grin that flashed wide in relief and welcome. Tip Johnson grabbed Breck's hand. "It's sure good to see you, Breck. I began to wonder if you got my letter."

"I did."

Two more men appeared in the moonlight, moving in from different directions. Their guns were holstered now.

Tip called to the men. "It's the boss. At last." He turned to Breck. "Let's get to the house, boy. Had supper?"

"In San Alma." Breck's voice still held an edge. "Funny kind of welcome, Tip."

They started walking toward the ranch house. Tip made an apologetic gesture. "We heard you coming and there was no hail for the house. We didn't know who it was."

"Still, you could have sung out instead of throwing bullets. Someone could have been hurt."

"And folks have been shot for doing just that," Tip said sharply. "It's been that way in San Alma for a long time now."

"I don't understand."

Tip spoke sadly. "Lots of things have happened since you've been gone, Breck. It'll take a long time to tell you. Wait until we get in the house."

They were now in the shadow of the building. Breck felt that his uncle would appear any moment on the porch saying a word of welcome in that gruff voice that had concealed real kindness and affection.

The illusion was dispelled as Tip spoke to one of the men. "Take his horse to the stable, Chuck. Unsaddle and feed it. Give him a hand, Lew."

As the two men started off, Breck called after them, "Come into the house later and we'll get acquainted."

He followed Tip across the porch. The foreman opened the door and disappeared into the dark room. Breck stepped inside and softly closed the door behind him. A match flared and Tip applied it to a lamp wick. He replaced the chimney and moved to the windows.

Breck felt as though he had stepped back ten years. Every piece of furniture in the long, low-ceilinged room was familiar. His eyes rested on the heavy, leather-covered chairs, the big square table on which the lamp sat, the doors leading to the other rooms, the stone fireplace at one end, and then Tip.

The foreman hastily moved to the windows and pulled the blinds. Tip Johnson looked as stocky and powerful as ever.

It seemed to Breck that the years had only deepened the wrinkles in the man's leathery face and added more gray to his shock of coarse, stubborn hair. Tip turned with a subtle air of relief that puzzled Breck. Now Breck could see that the years had left other marks on him. The brown eyes were more weary than Breck remembered, the flesh about the neck and jaw a bit flabby.

Tip grinned at Breck and studied him. "Filled out more, that's certain. Put on meat and muscle where it counts. Still got burrs under your saddle?"

Breck chuckled. "I lost most of them along the way."

"Settled down. Got your balance," Tip nodded. "Good thing, too, especially around these parts now."

He waved Breck to the chair Uncle Jim had always used. Breck sat down, sensing that in the little gesture, Tip had acknowledged Breck's right of control over the ranch. Breck *was* Circle M from this moment on, Tip's boss as Uncle Jim had been before.

Tip sat in a chair nearby and rubbed work-calloused palms together, still studying Breck and seeming to approve of what he saw. "I made things ready for you, Breck. Fixed up your old room, and Jim's, too. Didn't know which one you would want."

"Mine," Breck said quickly. "The other room . . . I don't know. It just wouldn't be right."

Tip made a slight gesture, but he was pleased. "Jim wouldn't mind. Always figured you'd take it over some day. But no rush."

Boots rapped across the porch. Tip instantly swung around, eyes narrowing as though he half expected enemies. A knock sounded on the door and the old man lost his tension. "That'll be the boys." His voice lifted. "Come in."

The two men entered. Tip introduced them. First Chuck Leyden, a fair-haired, steady-eyed man, competent and dependable. Breck judged him to be pressing forty and was pleased with the strong grip of his hand.

Lew Mannering, though physically Chuck's opposite, gave the same impression of competence. He was half a head shorter than Chuck, with swarthy skin and black hair that hinted of a strong Indian strain. He shook hands with a quiet "Howdy," and his eyes were as honestly weighing and appraising as Breck's. Breck instantly liked the men. Uncle Jim—or Tip—still had that old ability to pick good men.

Tip sighed. "This is the crew, Breck. Circle M doesn't need a dozen hands any more. Wish it did, but . . ." His voice drifted off, then lifted. "Aim to stay on?"

"Figured on it. I'm tired of roaming and working for

someone else. Besides, I think Uncle Jim wanted me to keep Circle M going."

"That's what he wanted," Tip agreed. He looked at the men. "Think you can work for him?"

Lew nodded and Chuck grinned and said, "Looks like he can fill Jim Malone's boots. I'll stay on as long as he does."

"That's fair enough," Tip answered. "Better hit your blankets. No telling how much work this'n will throw at us come morning. 'Night, boys."

Chuck and Lew threw approving looks at Breck and went to the door. He noticed that they opened it just wide enough to slip through and instantly closed it again. They apparently stood for long moments in the dark shadows beneath the porch roof because some time passed before Breck heard their steps quickly fading away.

His reception, Tip's caution about the blinds and the manner in which all of them obviously searched shadows before moving spoke of tension, of expected danger or attack.

Tip dropped back in his chair. "Chuck and Lew are top hands and men to ride the river with. Jim hired them about a year ago. The old crew was laid off over a period of years."

Breck frowned. "What's happening, Tip? Circle M was a good ranch ten years ago. Uncle Jim never wrote there was trouble. All of you act as though you expect to be bush-whacked any minute." He looked startled as a new thought hit him. "Was Uncle Jim—"

"No, he died in bed," Tip said. The stocky man paced to one of the windows, then to the table. "They never laid a hand on him, but I figure those outlaws killed Jim, just as certain as if they shot him."

"Outlaws? In San Alma?"

"Jim never said a word about it?"

"Nothing."

Tip bit at his lip. "That's a surprise. There's been nothing *else* to think about in San Alma the last five years." He shook his head. "It'd be like Jim, though, not to tell you. He'd figure it might bring you back in a hurry and Jim always said you had to ride your own trail in your own way. He wasn't the kind to yell for help."

"How come Jip Terry or the ranchers didn't drive the renegades out? And who are they?"

"Jip was gone three years before they showed their faces. At first, we'd only see one or two. Hardcases drifting through, we thought. Nothing to worry about. Nothing at all! It took us some time to catch on that the Jerry Hecker bunch had a hideout in the Thunder Range."

"The Hecker gang!" Breck exclaimed.

17

"There ain't no worse bunch of killers, robbers, rustlers and snakes, Breck. That's the bunch we got riding our backs. We finally caught on. Too late, then, but it took two killings and a shoot-up of the town for us to learn that. Now it's worth your life to even complain about them. It's damn near worth your life to go to town, for you never know when they'll decide they don't like the color of your eyes."

Breck stared. Tip read his thoughts. "No, Breck, we didn't lay down and roll over for them. Like I said, it was some time before we learned who the bunch was and where they hid out. When we did, we went to Roy Cantro." Tip made an angry grimace. "We might as well have howled at the moon for all the good it did us." His leathery face became dark and brooding. "We decided to chase them out ourselves. There were twenty of us and following sign was easy. None of us stopped to figure that they were pretty sure of themselves if they didn't cover the trail to their hideout. We found it, all right. Up in the Thunders." His eyes glinted. "Jerry Hecker had found a place up there an army couldn't get into. We tried. Five killed, half of us wounded by the time we pulled out of that canyon—the only way in."

Breck shook his head. It did not seem possible that the events Tip recounted could have happened in San Alma, but the harsh ring of Tip's voice could not be denied.

"That fight knocked the spunk out of most of us, and Jerry Hecker knew it. His renegades made the town and the whole valley theirs. Now and then they'd disappear and you could be sure they were out on some rustling job or bank or train holdup. Then they'd be back again with plenty of money for celebrating.

"Now and then someone would try to stand up to them. You could figure then that he'd catch a slug in the brisket, or he'd be rustled blind, or his ranch would burn down. There ain't many now that dare open their mouths."

"Uncle Jim knuckled under, too?" Breck asked.

"In a way. What else could he do? But now and then he'd speak his mind and it would get to Jerry Hecker. We began losing beef—just a little at first, as though warning us. Two of our hands got slickered into gun fights in town. Then we lost more cattle. I figure Hecker'd decided he'd had enough of Jim, so he planned to break us."

Tip dropped heavily into the chair. "He damn near has. Just two weeks before Jim died, we lost a hundred head in one clip. I think that was the thing that finished Jim. He could see Circle M going to pieces. He just gave up, Breck. He'd sit where you are and just stare out the window or he'd walk around the yard hardly noticing anything. He'd tell me

18

to handle everything, that he didn't care. I did, best I could."

Tip sighed. "I've heard stories that Indians could roll up in a blanket and will themselves to die. I swear that's what Jim did. Only one thing would make him perk up a little—you."

Breck raised his head as Tip continued. "He'd talk about the way you used to be. He'd tell me you was to have this ranch and then he'd say it wouldn't be worth the paper of the deed if we kept on losing beef. But he couldn't work himself up to fighting back, or even ranching. I wrote to you, hoping that if you came, Jim would get better."

"It took two months for that letter to find me, Tip."

"I knowed it was something like that." He shrugged. "Main thing now is you're here. I hope you stay, but I won't blame you one bit if you don't. In fact, I advise you to get what you can from Circle M and ride out."

Breck tried to digest all that Tip had told him, to understand the change that had come to San Alma. Now he knew that the feeling he had had about the men he had seen in town had been right. The Hecker gang. His frown deepened.

"It's hard to figure this, Tip. San Alma is the county seat. It has a sheriff and there's a court. Why didn't the law back you?"

"The law ain't helped anybody for five years, though it goes through all the motions."

"You mean the sheriff is in with the gang?"

"Not one of them, but in their pay. At first, Cantro rammrodded the town and county. If one of those hardcases tried to sink his spurs, he was in trouble. No doubt about that. Then things changed. Now and then Cantro arrests one of that bunch, but it's for some little thing. Maybe he'll throw a drunk in jail overnight or make him pay a small fine. It's like Cantro tries to show he's a real lawman, but it fools nobody.

"You can go to Cantro about a rustling. He'll ride out and pick up the trail and start following sign like he means to get those cows back. But nothing happens. He loses the trail. Say there's a gun killing in town, Cantro's right there in a hurry. But somehow he always finds out the killing was done in self-defense."

"It's hard to believe, Tip. Cantro came into Tres Cruces and showed no favors to anyone. He faced up to the bad bunch down there and he could notch his gun at least half a dozen times. This thing in San Alma doesn't sound like the Cantro I heard about."

Tip's lips set. "And that don't sound like the Cantro we

know up here. Ask around, you'll find out what it's like." He added, "That is, if you decide to stay."

Breck grinned crookedly. "You sound like you want me to leave."

Tip snorted. "You know better! But I know what you're up against. I say sell the spread for what you can get."

"How bad is it, Tip?"

"We can go over the ranch books tomorrow. But I can tell you there's not much beef left. It would be an uphill fight to bring Circle M back to what it was, even if the outlaws leave you alone. But they won't. The odds are all against you, Breck, much as I hate to say it."

Breck rose. "You should know, Tip, but I'd still like to see for myself before I make up my mind. We'll look it over come morning. Right now, a bed would look mighty fine to me."

Tip picked up the lamp and led the way down the familiar hallway to Breck's old room. He placed the lamp on the table and pulled down the blinds while Breck stood in the doorway, feeling the rush of memories.

Tip turned from the window. "I've told you what San Alma's like these days. A man keeps a gun close wherever he goes, whatever he does. You keep the windows covered at night. You keep your eyes and ears open."

"Sounds like the old Indian days."

"It's worse," Tip snapped. "Then, you knew where you stood with them. Now, the gent who buys you a drink this afternoon might help raid your ranch tonight or steal your beef tomorrow. Good night, Breck."

He was gone. Breck undressed slowly. He blew out the lamp and lay down on the bed. In the darkness, warm memories of the past warred with the heavy problems of the present, and it was a long time before he dropped off to sleep.

Breakfast was over just as the first gray streaks of dawn touched the sky. Breck went out in the yard with Tip, listening to his orders to Chuck and Lew.

By then, morning light was clear and Breck made a short inspection tour of the buildings with Tip. Breck was pleased with what he saw. The buildings, corrals and fences were in excellent condition.

The old man growled, "I wish you could say that of the rest of the spread. But you'll see."

Breck could not help his instinctive hesitation as he stepped into the small room that served as the ranch office. He felt like he was intruding on another man's domain as he seated himself at the desk and opened the first of the heavy ledgers.

The accounts revealed the steady deterioration of the Circle

M. Tip showed him tally books, and the diminishing head counts confirmed the ledger entries. Breck leaned back in the chair and, in a discouraged rhythm, tapped the tally book on the edge of the desk.

Tip stirred. "You can see how it is. Might be just enough stock left so you can manage to sell, if you can find someone who don't know what it's like in San Alma."

Breck looked at the worn, scuffed cover of the tally book. "And enough left so we've still got a chance to build up the herd."

"Don't forget that Hecker bunch."

"I'm not." His gray eyes held Tip's steadily. "You figure this is a long gamble and a poor business deal. You're advising me from your brain, Tip, not your heart."

Tip's eyes slid away slowly. "Everything of Uncle Jim's is in Circle M, Tip. He gave it to me. Maybe it's good business to get rid of it, but it's like leaving Uncle Jim in a tight."

Tip's voice became more burred. "He can't know."

"Maybe not. But I'd mind, Tip. I'd say we have a chance, a fighting one—at least from the tally."

"That's book count," Tip warned. "What's actually out on the range?"

"Let's find out," Breck said and stood up.

Breck sensed the old man's secret approval as they saddled up and rode out. Some of the gloom left his leathery face and he rode a little straighter in the saddle. They rode first toward the slopes of the Granadas that bound Circle M to the south. Then they moved westward at a steady pace.

Now and then they came on small bunches of cattle, made a quick count and rode on. Tip led the way up a draw or into a hidden grassy pocket in the hills where cattle were likely to graze. This was to be only an estimation. An experienced cowman could get a rough, but dependable, idea of the total herd based on the number actually encountered and tallied.

This quick count showed that the estimated loss on the ranch books was right. Breck's eyes became more clouded and Tip lost his spark of enthusiasm. Breck knew that the last roundup tally would be far over actual count, an indication that the Hecker gang still had a particular liking for Circle M beef.

Yet he felt he still had a chance. He knew that fear and appeasement of outlaws only added to their arrogance, and this had apparently happened in San Alma. It was one thing to rustle beef when you knew the risk was small, the pursuit halfhearted and fruitless. It would be quite another if you

21

risked a forty-four slug or rifle bullet and you knew the pursuit would be relentless.

It depended on Chuck and Lew, of course. Breck was certain of Tip. He needed only the word and a leader. So if Chuck's and Lew's undoubted loyalty extended to gunplay, the Hecker gang might find Circle M a cocklebur in their teeth.

Breck toyed with vague ideas and half plans. Their ride was steady and now they cut directly across the range to the north. The sun mounted high and Breck began to think of the sandwiches they had wrapped in their saddlebags. They'd eat, make a quick survey of this area and then return to the house. In the morning, they'd start preparing for an extra roundup to get an exact count.

Tip's surprised grunt brought Breck out of his reveries. The foreman pointed toward a low hummock. "Cook or branding fire, and I won't bet which."

A pencil of smoke lifted beyond the knoll. Breck shot a hard glance at Tip, who nodded grimly. They set spurs and rode directly for the knoll. They topped the rise and drew rein, narrowed eyes instantly centering on a fire several hundred yards out. A man squatted before it, holding a steak impaled on a running iron over the flames. Tip pointed off to the left.

A dead steer lay there and Breck could see the gaping wound in the flank. His eyes sparked and anger shook him. He rode slowly down the slope, heading for the dead animal.

The stranger's saddled horse, ground-tied a few feet beyond the fire, snorted. Instantly, the man jumped up and wheeled around. He made no effort to run but lifted his hat and made the circling motion that was a warning to "ride around and keep your distance."

The utter gall and arrogance of the man fanned Breck's cold fury. He was close enough to the dead cow now to see the Circle M brand. The man had deliberately killed it to have himself a steak.

Breck looked toward the man by the fire. Again the man waved him around and then took a defiant stance, legs slightly spread, right hand dropping to his holster.

Breck's pent-up anger exploded and he set spurs deep and hard. The horse lunged forward, heading directly for the man by the fire, who fell into a crouch as his hand slashed to his gun.

Breck dimly heard Tip's yell and the rolling pound of hoofs behind him.

Chapter III

BRECK'S COLT FLASHED into his hand and he snapped off a shot to hurry the renegade. A man on a racing horse has little chance of accuracy, so all the advantage lay with the man by the fire. He had merely to take that extra second needed to place the slug where he wanted. Breck's only chance was to rattle him.

He fired again as his spurs raked and the horse gave another burst of speed. Coals spurted from the fire where the bullet struck.

The renegade flinched and got off a hasty shot. It harmlessly split the air above Breck's head. Breck fired again as the renegade threw an alarmed look toward Tip, bearing down from another direction.

Breck savagely twisted the reins and the horse wheeled about. Breck fired as the black muzzle of the man's gun swung up toward him. His slug caught the man in the right shoulder and flung him half around as his gun flew from spasmodically opened fingers.

Breck vaulted from the saddle and ran toward the renegade, who now lay sprawled beyond the fire, stunned by the slamming force of the heavy slug. He kicked the man's gun far to one side.

He leveled his gun on the renegade as the man stirred and pulled himself to a sitting position. His right arm hung limp and dark blood stained his dirty, nondescript shirt. He touched his shoulder with his left hand and then stared in dull amazement at the red on his fingers.

"Get up," Breck ordered.

The man's head lifted and revealed a face that was all pinched together: close-set eyes, thin nostrils, pursed mouth barely covering protruding yellow teeth.

Tip glared at the renegade. "That's Red Hollings, one of Jerry Hecker's beauties."

Hollings glared at them. Breck gave the order again and Hollings spat to one side. "Go to hell."

Breck's gun roared and the slug smashed the spur on the renegade's boot. Breck spoke through tight, thin lips. "The next one will bury you. Get on your feet—now!"

Hollings' slitted eyes showed a slight gleam of fear that

was swiftly gone. He pulled himself to his feet, holding his shoulder. The numbing shock of the bullet still deadened his nerves, so he felt no pain. He threw a venomous glance at Tip and deliberately turned and started toward his horse.

Breck took a lunging stride, grabbed his uninjured shoulder and spun him around. Hollings snarled, "Better let me ride off before you get in more trouble."

"Trouble!" Breck exploded. "What do you think you're in?"

"Nothing my friends can't fix up. You'll wish to hell you'd rode around once they hear about it."

"They'll hear, and plenty," Breck snapped. "You make another wrong move and your friends will bury you."

Hollings started to grin and then the first shock of pain struck. He grimaced and his fingers tightened on his wound. Breck spoke over his shoulder. "Hold your gun on him, Tip. I'll patch him up, little as he deserves it."

He ordered Hollings to unbutton his shirt. A quick glance told Breck the slug had probably flattened against a bone, breaking it. Beads of sweat showed on Hollings' forehead and the fight went out of him as pain gripped hard.

Breck staunched the flow of blood as best he could, then ripped the man's shirt into long pieces to make an improvised sling. By the time he finished, Hollings sat on the ground again, pursy lips writhing.

While Tip held his gun on the prisoner, Breck walked to the fire and lifted the running iron with the hunk of charred meat on the end of it. He looked toward the dead steer— several hundred pounds of valuable animal killed in order to get a pound or so of steak. Breck flung the ruined meat off the iron and turned back to the prisoner.

He held up the long rod. "Sign of a rustler and against the law. Circle M beef killed just to fill your worthless belly. Let's see what the sheriff has to say about this. On your horse."

Breck thought he saw a momentary amused gleam in the man's eyes, but Hollings, wincing with the pain in his shoulder, pulled himself to his feet and walked slowly toward his horse.

Breck spoke to Tip. "Skin the brand off that steer. We'll show it to Cantro."

"You're wasting time," Tip growled. "Shoot or hang this jasper here and now."

Hollings stopped with a jerk. Breck shook his head. "Lynching's no good. We'll take him in."

It was late afternoon by the time the three men rode into San Alma's main street. Hollings swayed and clung to the saddlehorn with his one good hand, his face gray and twisted.

24

Tip had long ago taken the reins and now led the renegade's horse while Breck rode slightly to the rear.

As they neared the first buildings, a man came out of a gun shop, stared and then wheeled back inside. He reappeared with three more men who stared after the riders and then followed cautiously along the street.

They circled the courthouse. Ahead and to the right, stood the sheriff's office and jail. Across the street, Breck saw men loafing on the porch of the Cattleman Saloon. They lined the rail as Breck, Tip and the wounded renegade came closer. Suddenly one of them darted inside.

Tip turned in at the sheriff's office and swung out of the saddle as Breck rode up on the other side of Hollings. The renegade looked up with pain-glazed eyes as Breck's harsh voice ordered, "Get down."

There was no fight left in Hollings. He swung his leg over the saddle and gasped with pain as his fingers lost their grip on the horn. He tumbled, to be caught by Tip, who roughly steadied him.

The three pushed into the sheriff's office, Breck paying no attention to the gathering, buzzing crowd before the stores and saloons. He swung open the door and shoved Hollings inside.

Cantro sat behind his desk, oiling a gun. He looked up as the door opened and jumped to his feet when Hollings catapulted inside, caught himself on the edge of the desk and hung there until Breck pulled him back and down into a chair.

Cantro's jaw hung open, then closed with an almost audible snap. "What is this?"

Tip dropped the square of hide bearing the Circle M brand on the desk. Breck briefly told what had happened, his voice holding a slight tremor of renewed anger. Cantro looked from one to the other, then down at Hollings, his lips pulled tight.

"That's it," Breck finished. "Running iron. Illegal. Destruction and theft of property. That ought to put him away for a few years."

"You and Tip saw it?" Cantro asked.

"We came on him. Caught him in the act."

Cantro's knuckles hit the desk with a sharp rap. "That's enough to jail him, Malone. It's time we stopped this sort of thing around here. I can promise you he'll come to trial damn fast."

He turned and lifted a big ring of keys from a wall peg. Hollings made a whispered moan, swayed. Breck glanced at him. "That shoulder ought to be patched."

Cantro hesitated, nodded. "I'll get Doc Vance to look at

him before we throw him in a cell. Keep an eye on him. I'll be right back."

He hurried out. Breck, surprised, looked at Tip, who shrugged. Hollings moaned again and then Breck saw a worn couch against one wall. With Tip's help, he moved Hollings to it and the man collapsed, eyes closed.

The street door opened and Breck wheeled around. His face lighted. "Doc!"

The man was short, thin and wiry, with shaggy gray brows and unruly hair. He shifted the black bag to his left hand and thrust his right at Breck. Brown eyes, circled by deep pouches, became brighter and gentle lips, under a mustache as shaggy as the brows, broke into a pleased smile. His voice sounded like the impatient snapping of dry twigs.

"Breck, damn glad to see you. But no time now. That the patient?" At Breck's nod, he stepped to the couch, opened the renegade's shirt. A single look and he opened his black bag and went to work.

Someone else in San Alma who hasn't changed, Breck thought as he watched the old man's nimble, sure fingers. He started to speak but Doc Vance cut him short. "Talk later, Breck. Busy. Broken shoulder, loss of blood, slug's gotta come out."

Cantro came in. He threw a glance at Breck but said nothing. There was a subtle change in his attitude, a new surety.

At last Doc Vance stood up. "You can move him now. He'll live, worse luck."

Cantro picked up the ring of keys and, with Breck's and Tip's help under Doc's explosive directions, Hollings was carried back to a cell, placed on a bunk and securely locked in. They all returned to the office.

Doc snapped his bag shut and rolled down his sleeves. "Who shot him?"

"I did," Breck said.

"You must be pretty gun-fast. Hollings claims a bunch of notches. Killed a man in San Alma not long ago. Where'd you learn such shooting?"

"The Mexican border. A lot of trouble down there, one way or another. You learn to shoot fast or die."

"Looks like you ought to be a lawman."

Breck laughed at the peppery doctor. "No thanks. I've got enough worries as it is."

Doc Vance grunted. "Left a patient at the office. I've got to get back. Will you be in town awhile? Want a chance to talk like a friend, not a doctor."

Breck grinned. "I'll stay around, say, at the Thunder Saloon?"

26

"If I get a chance, I'll be over."

The peppery little man picked up his bag and, with a brief nod to all of them, left the office. Breck chuckled and turned to Tip. "Let's cut the dust from our throats."

Cantro spoke up. "Malone, you'd be smart if you forgot that drink and just pulled out." He shook his head when Breck stared hard at him. "Man, I'm thinking of your own good. Red Hollings has friends in town and they might want to even the tally for him. It would be wise to stay out of sight until they cooled down."

Breck's gray eyes were level. "Are there many of them?"

"Plenty."

"Then they must be the same breed of cat—rustlers, thieves, gunmen. Why are they allowed to stay?"

Cantro's face subtly lengthened and his black eyes held steady. Then his wide grin flashed. "Doc was right. You *would* make a lawman!"

"Hardly, but I still wonder about that bunch of hardcases."

Cantro's smile vanished and his voice held a note of regret. "Malone, I'd be the first to chase 'em out if they gave me a reason. But there's no charges against them in this county. Now and then they get a little noisy, but they've committed no crimes I can prove, or anyone else, either. I don't like them, Malone, but they've got as much right to be in town as you or me."

Breck spoke dryly. "But you want *me* to get out."

"For your own good, man, that's all. I can't and won't order you, just hope. I figured you'd help me avoid trouble."

Breck searched the strangely pale face with the striking dark eyes. He read sincerity and then recalled what Tip had said about the lawman. "We'll see. I don't like to run."

"Run! Man, it would be doing me a favor!"

Breck turned to the door. Tip followed him out and they stopped at the edge of the canopied porch. Most of the crowd had dispersed, but Breck noticed that the porch of the Cattleman Saloon was filled. From this distance, the men looked cut from the same bolt of cloth as Hollings.

Tip broke in on his thoughts, his voice filled with sarcasm. "Cantro's sure worried about our hides. He'll probably stay up nights, to hear him tell it. Aim to ride out?"

"I still want a drink and a talk with Doc Vance. The Thunder good enough?"

Tip glanced toward the Cattleman. "Not as crowded. One thing, Breck. Cantro was right thinking trouble might start. Be ready for it."

They went to the Thunder. The few men in the place looked sharply at Breck and Tip, then away again. None bore the outlaw stamp and one smiled, started to say something, then threw an alarmed look at the batwings and moved away.

Breck and Tip sat at one of the tables and gave their order. Breck looked about and caught more than one pair of eyes sliding away. Soon a man rose from one of the tables and left. In a moment, two more found their way to the batwings and out. Gradually the place emptied.

"People don't like our company," Breck said shortly.

"They like it," Tip corrected, "but they're afraid of it— until they know what Jerry Hecker aims to do."

Just then, Tom Wheeler came in, turned to their table and leaned on it. "Heard what happened. I figure this is another drink on the house."

Breck smiled. "You keep that up, you'll go broke."

Tom straightened. "Not a chance. You won't live that long."

He walked behind the bar, took off his frock coat and tied on a white apron. Then he brought a bottle to the table. "Help yourselves," he said.

Tip poured drinks for Breck and himself and lifted his glass. "To a longer life than Tom allows us."

The batwings swung open and Doc Vance stepped in. He saw them, spoke over his shoulder to someone still on the porch, and came to the table. Another man entered. He was tall and powerful, the iron-gray of his hair a fitting symbol of the iron strength of his body. A battered Stetson sat on the back of his head, revealing a face as craggy and square as the rocks of the Thunder Range.

Doc, now at the table, looked back at the other man and waved his hand toward Breck. "Matt, remember this ranny? He's got growed up and gun-fast since you last saw him."

Breck came to his feet, eyes alight, as the older man came up. They clasped hands and Breck said softly, "Matt Unger. Sure glad to see you again. I swear you and Doc haven't changed a bit."

"Older, and Doc's got more twists in his tail," Unger grinned, then sobered. "Doc says you brought in Red Hollings. What happened?"

Breck poured drinks around. He noticed that Tom Wheeler had gone to the batwings and was looking out on the street. He forgot him when, at Unger's insistence, he retold how Hollings had been taken.

Unger listened, throwing a sharp look at Doc Vance now and then. Unger was a heavy-featured man with a pendulous lower lip that he tugged on now and then as he listened.

When Breck finished, Doc Vance leaned toward Matt. "Well?"

Unger grunted and stood up, looking toward the door.

"Quite a story. First that's happened in these parts for a long time." He looked down at Breck. "We're still next-door neighbors. Jim used to drop over a lot before. . . ." His voice drifted, caught. "I wish you would, too—say, first of the week?"

"I'd like that fine, Matt."

"I'll look for you, without fail."

Doc Vance finished his drink and rose, grumbling. "Got to get back. Don't get a chance to act human. Always have to grab a word and a drink on the run. See you later, Breck."

He hurried out after Unger, who turned at the door, looking back. "See you next week."

Breck nodded and the batwings whispered. Tom walked slowly back behind the bar. Breck frowned, recalling now that some of Unger's questions had been sharp. And that invitation—he sensed something more than friendliness under it.

He glanced at Tip, who moodily studied his whiskey glass. The batwings whispered again and Breck looked up. Two men stood there. Men with holsters tied low to their right legs, men with the harsh assurance of their gun speed. One was fair, one dark, but they came to the table with the same panther-like stride, the same half grin.

Gunslingers, Breck thought, and rose. Tip's chair scraped back as he stood up, hand dropping close to his holster. Only the flick of their eyes disclosed that the two men had seen the movement. They halted a few feet away.

The dark one spoke. "Which of you gents shot Red Hollings?"

Breck kept his voice level. "I did."

"You?" he said. He studied Breck carefully, then looked at his companion. "Will you remember him?"

"Sure."

The dark one grinned crookedly at Breck. "Thanks."

They turned and walked out, leaving Breck and Tip staring blankly after them. Breck heard a deep sigh of relief from the bar and saw that Tom Wheeler leaned against it, the twin barrels of a shotgun barely showing above the mahogany. He hastily concealed the weapon.

Breck caught his voice. "Some of the Hecker bunch?"

"That's right," Tom said.

Breck eased down in his chair and looked at his foreman. "Now what do you make of that?"

"I can't . . . it worries me. Boy, this is just a sample of what it's like here. Now what about keeping the Circle M?"

Breck's jaw tightened. "I'm not used to running."

"They'll pressure you," Tip warned. "Bushwhack, gun trap,

rustling, raids, burning—that's just a few of the cards in their deck. You can see how they start to work on a man."

Breck smacked his palm on the narrow chair arm. "And we've started. With Red Hollings."

"Think Cantro will do anything there? Remember, he tried to get you to leave."

"Damned if I'll run out of town and damned if I'll run from the ranch—at least, not yet."

"Boy, you're a fool," Tip said, but there was admiration in his voice.

Breck glanced at the clock. "We've stayed long enough. They know we're not scared. Let's head back to the ranch."

Tip followed Breck to the door. They stepped out on the porch, eyes casting about sharply for the two gunhawks. Breck's hand was close to his holster and Tip's leathery face was grim and tight.

Breck instantly became aware of the group before the sheriff's office. His eyes widened in stunned surprise as he saw Red Hollings being helped onto his horse while Cantro and some men looked on.

With an angry oath, Breck strode down the steps, Tip at his side. As they approached the jail, there was a murmur among the crowd.

Tip spoke in a low, tight voice. "Watch for a gun trap."

Breck's angular face was harsh, anger showing in the set of his jaw and lips. His eyes centered on Cantro as he came to a halt a few feet away. He indicated Hollings, who managed a mocking, pain-twisted grin. "I thought that man was under arrest."

Cantro smiled easily. "The court freed him."

"The court?" Breck exploded. "Without trial?"

"But there was a trial." Cantro indicated the man beside him. "Judge Tracy held a special session and Hollings waived a jury."

Judge Tracy cleared his throat and Breck's blazing eyes swung to him. The man had once been handsome and Breck dimly recognized in the blurred line of jaw and chin and bloodshot eyes the features of a young and promising attorney of ten years ago. Now, though he wore a fine black suit and held a cigar between fleshy fingers, the tracery of veins about the broad nose and the unhealthy puffiness of the face revealed a man more interested in the bottle than in law books.

He stood a little straighter as he spoke. "The San Alma court is noted for its desire to mete swift justice to lawbreakers. When I heard this man was accused of rustling, I immediately called him to trial."

Breck's voice shook. "Why wasn't I called then?"

"You could not be found, sir. The sheriff presented the case for the prosecution. Under my own direct examination, I found that neither you nor Mr. Johnson, your foreman, could call up any supporting witnesses to your complaint."

"But we caught this man in the very act!"

"So you say," Tracy nodded, "and I congratulate Sheriff Cantro for vigorously presenting your side. But there was only your word against that of the defendant, who produced some impeachable character witnesses. They convinced the court that he is not the caliber of man to descend to so low a crime. Since there was grave doubt that he actually committed the crime, I could not find him guilty. The court so ordered and Mr. Hollings is released."

Breck's gray eyes narrowed and glittered. Judge Tracy's watery eyes shifted. Then he drew himself up. "I can understand your anger, Malone, but I suggest that you do not allow it to lead you into contempt of court. As I have said, Mr. Hollings had excellent character witnesses."

"Character! Him?" Breck shouted. "Now who could—"

"I could, Mr. Malone."

A man slightly behind and to one side of the judge stepped forward. He was slender, half a head shorter than Breck. A pearl-gray derby topped a round, pleasant face. Flecked hazel eyes danced with amusement as he extended a slender hand. Thin lips smiled widely under the pencil line of a black mustache.

"I know Red Hollings' character very well," he said. "I'm Jerry Hecker."

Chapter IV

BRECK COULD ONLY STARE, amazed at the man's utter gall, unable to reconcile this smiling person with the outlaw of whom he had heard so much. He read the wolflike amusement lurking in the flecked eyes.

"Outlaw stands character for outlaw?" Breck demanded.

Hecker dropped his hand without seeming to notice it had not been accepted. "Who in this town would call me an outlaw, or doubt my word?"

"I would," Breck said.

A hulking man behind Hecker growled deep in his throat and swayed forward. Hecker's slender hand stopped him. His smile remained and the flecked eyes showed no anger. "Leave be, Chulo. Mr. Malone has yet to know how things go in San Alma."

"I know enough that—" Breck started.

Cantro moved between Breck and Hecker, his eyes level and heavy with warning. He swung around to Hecker. "I'll vouch for Malone. With Jim dying and all, he's a little touchy right now."

"I understand." Hecker spoke directly to the sheriff. "None of you need worry about Red. I'll see to it that he stays on his own range."

"A troublemaker," Cantro said.

"I can cure that." Hecker's smile lost its warmth. He glanced at. the big man beside him. "Chulo, we'd better take Red home, just to make sure he's learned his lesson."

"Then you admit—" Breck broke in.

Hecker moved beyond the sheriff. "Admit what, Mr. Malone? Judge Tracy cleared Red and that's good enough." His smile flashed again. "I hope next time we meet there'll be nothing between us."

He walked toward the Cattleman Saloon. Chulo, thumbs hooked in his gunbelt, gave Breck a long, scowling scrutiny. Then he followed after Hecker.

Breck looked after the pair, his lips pressed, his gray eyes cold and glittering. Tip spoke softly. "It's a wolf trap. Don't walk in it. Nothing would suit 'em better."

Just then, Judge Tracy stepped down from the sheriff's porch. He moved with dignity, but the puffy skin and bleary eyes that hopefully searched Breck's face quickly destroyed the illusion.

He spoke affably. "Malone, I remember you as a spirited young rannihan kicking high and handsome. It's a pleasure to have you back, sir."

Breck asked, "You're a judge now?"

Tracy's chest came out. "That's right."

"Whose judge?"

The man drew himself up. "What do you mean by that?"

"I remember people saying you were a lawyer with a lot of promise. I would hardly have known you."

Tracy's face paled and his lips shook. Cantro touched Breck's elbow, indicating the office. "Let's talk inside. Too many out here to watch and listen."

"Good idea," Tip agreed. Breck reluctantly turned toward the building, ignoring Tracy as though the man no longer existed. Cantro let Breck and Tip precede him and then closed the door. He took off his hat and blew his lips with relief as he dropped into his chair. "Breck, we near had two Malones in Boothill."

"Is that all you have to say?"

"It's enough!" Cantro retorted. "Jerry Hecker's small and looks soft, but don't let that fool you. Chulo Wyeth is a damned savage who enjoys killing. Only Hecker can keep him in line. I'm glad nothing started out there."

"What about Red Hollings?"

Cantro shrugged. "Judge Tracy ordered him released. There was nothing else I could do. You have to believe that."

Breck considered him a long moment and then stood up. "I believe you, Sheriff," he said, with dry sarcasm, and strode out before Cantro could reply.

Tip followed him. Their horses still stood at the sheriff's rack and Breck swung into the saddle in angry silence. He caught Tip's searching, worried look. They circled the court-house and at last the town was behind them. Tip had said nothing before, but now, out on the open range, he obviously felt relieved.

"We should have strung Hollings up."

"I figured the law would handle him."

"Judge Tracy? Give him a bottle and he'll decide any way you want it. What kind of law is that?"

Breck had no answer. Tip growled deep in his throat. "That Hecker bunch can't be touched. They murder and rob and Tracy frees 'em. They can't be tried again and there's nothing can be done."

Breck spoke thoughtfully. "Sure? If enough people worked together, Hecker's bunch wouldn't have much of a chance."

Tip sighed. "We thought of that. A couple of times. But those who talked about it died sudden and hard. A man has to figure the chance of a bullet between the eyes if he makes the first move. That can be discouraging."

Breck couldn't quite agree with Tip's hopeless summary. In the days that followed, he did not forget the farcical trial of Red Hollings but the problems of the spread pushed it to the back of his mind. He had to make a decision about Circle M—stay on, or sell—and only an exact tally of the beef could give him the answer.

He worked with Tip, Chuck and Lew, moving from section to section of the ranch, combing each area. It was hard, grueling work and, as the days passed, Breck grimly realized that the actual tally was well below book count—proof that the outlaws had hit hard. But not so hard as Uncle Jim had thought. There was still a slim, fighting chance that Circle M might be rebuilt. Breck knew the odds were so long that it frightened him to consider them. He understood why Tip, despite his loyalty, had suggested he sell out.

That made sense. But Breck felt there was something else that also made sense. Jerry Hecker's bunch had, figuratively, killed Uncle Jim. Now if Breck gave up without a struggle, the outlaws' hold on the San Alma country would be strengthened just that much more. To run without a fight was unthinkable.

He and Tip finished the count in an area within easy riding distance of the town. They sat their horses at the foot of a long slope leading from the crest of a grassy knoll.

Tip looked at the final figure, his leathery features lengthening. "We've been stolen blind!"

Breck closed the tally book, his angular face tight and thoughtful. "Think we ought to give up?"

Tip grimaced. "I'll ride along whatever trail you take. One thing sure, you got to figure on the wild bunch. When could a rustler ever leave a cow alone? Most important, you didn't exactly fill Hecker and his bunch with joy and friendship the other day. Knowing you, I'd say you never will."

Breck grinned tightly, but made no comment. Tip studied the land. "It was a good spread, Breck. Still could be, but that ain't in the cards. You've got your choice of selling it now or going broke later."

"I don't like running." Breck lifted the reins. "But we can't decide here."

A rider suddenly appeared against the sky on the crest of the knoll. Breck's hand dropped to his holster. Then he realized the rider was a woman.

She sat the horse straight and proud, then came down the slope at a slow, assured pace.

"Hallie Yates," Tip said swiftly. "Lives in town and takes long rides by herself."

The woman reined in a few feet away and now Breck saw that she had a dark, sultry beauty. There was something bold in the way her dark eyes studied him and in her full, red lips. Her cheekbones were high, planing her smooth cheeks.

She wore a full, dark purple riding skirt with a short matching jacket over a white blouse that was demure enough, but still managed to lead the eye to the rounded curves of the full breasts. Her bonnet was also a dark purple, relieved by a small white feather. Raven-black hair swirled from beneath it to be caught up in a series of ringlets at the back of her neck.

Her voice was low, but clear and musical. "I think you're Breck Malone." She gave Tip a glance and turned again to Breck. "I never met Jim Malone but I heard a great deal about him. It was all good."

"Thank you, ma'am."

"I'm Hallie Yates." She added, with a crooked smile, "I have no doubt you'll hear of me—none of it good."

Surprise showed on Breck's face, but he spoke gravely. "Glad to meet you, Miss Yates."

She studied him and Breck grew uncomfortable under her close scrutiny. She smiled, and it was amazing how it lighted her face. "Sorry to be so curious, but there's talk of you in town."

"Word gets around," Breck said dryly.

"It's bound to. San Alma's small. Will you run the Circle M?"

It was his turn to stare, half in anger. She met his hard scrutiny squarely. "I'm too curious, I suppose."

"That's right."

"A fault of mine." She looked across the grassy range. "I've heard Jim Malone didn't want to live any more. The outlaws did that to him. A bullet's not the only way to kill a man."

"What are you trying to say?"

"I'm sorry for Jim Malone, that's all, and . . . hope nothing like that happens to you." She lifted the reins. "A pleasure to have met you and—good luck, whatever you do."

She wheeled the horse and raced back up the slope. She whipped over the crest of the hill and was gone. Breck stared blankly at Tip. "Now what do you make of that!"

"A warning, and nothing else."

"From her?"

"She's close to Roy Cantro."

"His girl?"

Tip scowled at the empty crest of the hill. "She lives on the north edge of San Alma, where the road leads toward the Thunders. She's a dressmaker and all the town ladies go to her. There's gossip about her and Cantro, but nothing definite."

"She knows a lot for a seamstress."

"Ain't that a fact! Where would she get it, except from Cantro?"

The next day, Breck felt they all deserved to rest their saddles and muscles. He himself did little more than wander around the ranch yard as an escape from long hours of going over the books, trying to marshal all the facts that would lead to a final decision.

The ranch books seemed to give but one answer: Circle M was dying on its feet, if not already dead. He would be wise to sell immediately, while he still might get a price within reason, but Breck could not quite bring himself to the final, irrevocable decision.

There was too much of his past here, too much of Uncle Jim's hopes, too much of Tip's hard sweat and labor. Figures alone could not give the full answer. Breck had known of too many men who had gritted their teeth in the face of reason, and won. He had known just as many who had lost, wry caution told him.

He should ride into San Alma, place the sale of the ranch in the banker's hands and leave. But he would sell out Tip's loyalty, and that of Chuck and Lew, who had kept the place until he could claim his inheritance. Nor did Breck want to feel the silent accusation of his uncle's memory for the rest of his life. There was also the matter of handing Jerry Hecker an intangible but, nonetheless, definite triumph.

So Breck was glad that a strange rider brought him out of his mental turmoil. The man rode for Matt Unger in San Alma for supplies, and brought a note for Breck on his way home.

It was from Alice Dane. She reminded Breck of his promise to pay her and her father a visit and scolded him for not having done so. She promised to forgive him if Breck would come for supper this very day.

Tip worriedly watched him. Breck grinned. "A pretty girl wants to see me, Tip. Reckon I'd better get slickered up?"

"Alice Dane?"

"How did you know?"

"I remember how she was about you ten years ago. Damn right you get slicked up! There's a lot worse fillies in this

36

world than Alice—and you can take that from an old hard-shelled bachelor."

"Yes, boss," Breck said mockingly.

Breck rode off looking forward to the next few hours. He felt as though he had pushed time back ten years as he rode up to the Dane house. The door opened and Alice came to the edge of the porch, waved to him.

"Stable your horse, Breck. We're waiting for you."

The same old greeting, he thought as he saw to his horse. He half expected her to come running to meet him as she used to do. But she did not appear and he felt a touch of disappointment.

As he left the stable, Alice appeared in the back door. "If you don't mind the kitchen, come in."

As he stepped up on the small porch, she looked up at him, radiant. "Breck, I wondered if you'd ever visit us again. It's good to have you back."

She turned before he could reply and he followed her inside, across the familiar spacious kitchen and dining room into the big main room, where a series of windows admitted the soft, golden rays of the setting sun.

Like the other rooms, this one seemed not to have changed. From the faded Brussels carpet on the floor to the horsehide sofa, the heavy rocker and the table with the ornate lamp, everything was as he had seen it last.

"Dad, here's Breck," Alice said.

Breck saw the black silhouette of a man against one of the windows, but Frank's voice came from the left. "A long time since we've seen you, Breck."

Frank Dane had always been tall and slender, but now his shoulders were rounded, his cheeks thin and pale. His sandy hair had receded and his eyes were sunken deep under ridged brows. He smiled, but there was reserve in his sharp probing look.

Breck shook hands and Dane indicated the figure by the window. "Do you know our sheriff, Roy Cantro?"

"We've met," Cantro said easily.

Breck hid his surprise. Cantro's smile was open and friendly. He held out his hand and apparently did not notice Breck's split-second hesitation. Cantro looked at Alice.

"She told me a lot about you, Malone, and your uncle, too."

Breck murmured something appropriate, very much aware of the possessive way in which Cantro regarded Alice. It was in the smile, in the assured way in which he spoke to Breck, as though he were Cantro's guest as well as the Danes'. Breck wondered how well Cantro was established in this household.

Alice suggested the men had time for one drink and then she would serve the meal. Frank Dane poured the whiskey and the talk was general at first. Breck sensed strain and reserve in Frank. It could have been caused by ten years' absence, but there was something more. Dane asked about his wanderings, but with no real interest. Now and then he would glance at Cantro, as though making certain of the lawman's approval. Breck was relieved when Alice called them to the table.

The meal was excellent and, for a time, Breck forgot his uneasiness. Conversation moved lightly, touching people Breck had known, and in a short time he had caught up with most of the history of San Alma. Cantro joined in and, for a time, there was a real warmth about the table.

Alice lightly and unwittingly shattered it. "How is the ranch, Breck?"

Dane's eyes instantly grew distant. Cantro continued to smile, but Breck sensed a sharpness under it. He made a slight grimace. Alice frowned, concerned. "That bad? I knew Uncle Jim had lost cattle, but no one knew exactly how hard he was hit."

"Nearly rustled blind," Breck said shortly. "No wonder he just gave up."

Dane stirred uncomfortably. "He wasn't the only one."

"So I hear. I wondered why something wasn't done about it—until the other day."

There was an immediate chill. Dane withdrew even further. Alice glanced sharply at Cantro, who sat very still, his smile vanishing. "Malone, I was on the rustlers' trail every time your uncle called me in. I hunted the canyons and draws. I did all I could. What more could be asked?"

"I don't know," Breck said slowly. "When I left, San Alma was peaceful and prosperous. Now Jerry Hecker and his bunch have the run of the town."

"You blame me?" Cantro asked quietly.

"I remember Tres Cruces."

Cantro flushed. "So do I. You knew where you stood in that town."

"And here?" Breck asked softly.

Dane suddenly stood up. "This is like arguing about the weather when all you can do is put up with it. We can't legally run Hecker's bunch out. They're here and they have to be lived with. If Roy can't handle the situation, no one can."

Cantro chuckled mirthlessly. "I wouldn't say that, Frank."

He moved to Alice's chair, helping her to rise. He held her hand and looked across the table at Breck.

"There's a lot here you don't understand. You're bound to make a few mistakes until you catch on." Alice made a slight move to disengage her hand, but Cantro held on to it, still looking at Breck. "Different, of course, once you know how things are and still make wrong moves. Then a man just asks for trouble."

He obviously spoke of the situation in San Alma, but, in the possessive way he stood by Alice, Breck sensed yet another meaning.

Breck had received a double warning.

Chapter V

THE NEXT MORNING, in the ranch office, Breck gnawed on two more problems and waited impatiently for Tip to come there after assigning work to the hands. He swung around as Tip entered and dropped into a chair. The old man grinned. "How was your courting?"

"What gave you that idea?" Breck asked sourly.

"I figured the wind blew in that direction."

"Roy Cantro was there."

Tip's leathery face registered disappointment. "I'd heard he'd been sashaying around her."

"You said he and Hallie Yates are pretty close."

"You see signs of it, but there ain't no proof. I'll bet my hat Alice don't know about that sewing woman."

"But Frank must! Why doesn't he tell her?"

"That's something you'd better ask Frank." Tip looked accusingly at Breck. "None of this would've happened if you hadn't rode yonderly. No blame to her if she looks for someone else."

"I didn't come back to get married."

"Fine. Then what her and Cantro do is their business."

Breck glared, exasperated, unable to reply. His hand moved over the chair arm in irritation. "About Cantro—how did he and Jip Terry get along?"

"No trouble. They respected one another."

"Then Cantro had to be the good lawman he was in Tres Cruces. Something happened to change him. You said it was about three years from the time the first renegade showed up until you went after the gang in the Thunders?"

"That's right."

"What about Cantro, at first?"

Tip searched the past, spoke slowly. "Breck, I heard tell that Cantro warned the first one out, and the gent skedaddled. Then there was a shoot-out, and the second was buried. A couple come riding in some time later, figuring on Cantro's scalp. Cantro killed one and the other lit out and run. Hank Owens—used to be the blacksmith—was killed by a stray bullet."

"Now *that* sounds like the Roy Cantro I heard about. What next?"

"There was some talk about Hank being killed because the sheriff was too quick to pull a gun. But that died down. Then merchants got mad when Cantro run a hardcase out of one of the stores."

"Why?"

"I heard he had just given a big order to Frank Dane and was paying for it when Cantro came in and told the man to pick up his money and get. Frank was hopping mad and got the other merchants worked up. Some talk of getting a new lawman. Then that blew over. A few more drifted in and out, but so long as they kept peaceful, Cantro left 'em alone. Then, as time went on, we found we had a wild bunch."

"And Cantro was re-elected?"

"That's right. Mostly town vote. Tracy was made judge same time. Right after that, real trouble started. I told you how Cantro acted and what we tried to do."

Breck nodded. Tip started in surprise from his chair and looked out the window. "Doc Vance! What's he doing here?"

Breck saw the horse and buggy swing toward the house. He strode to the front of the house and threw wide the door as Doc Vance's fist was lifted to pound on it. "Come in, Doc."

"No time. Making calls out this way and had to drop by." He looked accusingly at Breck. "You haven't visited Matt Unger like you promised."

"Doc, I've been too busy."

"Hmmmph! Well, be there tomorrow night for sure."

"Something wrong, Doc?"

"Wrong? What would there be? Just a poker game, and the first night off I've had in a month. Not often *that* happens. I want to pleasure myself with a drink or two and find out what you've been doing these ten years past. Can you be there?"

"Sure."

"Good. Right now I've got a fever waiting for me at the Running W. See you tomorrow."

He bobbed his head and Breck watched him hurry to his buggy and climb in. He wheeled the battered vehicle around and rattled out of the yard in a cloud of dust.

Breck laughed. "I swear that's the same rig he used ten years ago."

"It is," Tip said dryly. "Everybody makes bets when the contraption will just fall apart." He sobered. "Breck, we need staples—flour, sugar, things like that."

41

"I'll run into town and get 'em. Maybe the ride will clear my mind."

Breck hitched a team to the buckboard and drove into San Alma, arriving there about noon. The streets were deserted except for a few horses at the saloon hitchracks and in front of the small courthouse. Breck pulled in before Dane's store and tied the horses.

Roy Cantro came out. The sheriff stopped in surprise and then nodded in a friendly manner. His dark eyes cut to the buckboard. "Supplies?"

"Crew and me has to eat."

"Then you're staying on?"

"Why is everyone so blamed anxious to know?"

"Anxious?" Cantro laughed. "It's only friendly interest."

Breck gave him a sharp look. "As a friend, how would you feel if I stayed?"

"Why, I'd wish you luck. You'd need it. Should I?"

"I haven't decided yet."

Cantro started away but swung around when Breck called him. "The other night you said you knew where you stood in Tres Cruces."

"Did I?" Cantro's eyes suddenly turned sharp. "You have a better memory than me."

He walked away. Obviously, he did not want to be reminded of a slip of the tongue. Breck watched him cross the street, then thoughtfully turned into the store. He gave his order and told the clerk to put it on the buckboard. He then went to the Thunder, thinking that if Tom Wheeler were alone, he might give Breck further details on the change that had come to San Alma.

But Tom was not on duty when Breck entered the saloon. Three strangers stood at the far end of the bar. Their conversation broke off sharply as he came up and ordered. Then they dismissed him and continued their talk in low tones.

Breck stood alone, facing the ancient mirror and the row of bottles before it. He took a swallow of his drink and his thoughts turned to Cantro. What had changed him into an outlaw's cat's-paw?

The batwings whispered and Breck looked up into the mirror. He saw Chulo Wyeth's hulking figure first and then the slender, dapper shape of Jerry Hecker. Breck placed his glass on the bar, freeing his right hand.

Hecker looked at Breck's reflection in apparent surprise. He still wore the derby hat, the neat coat and white shirt. His teeth flashed in a smile as he came up beside Breck. Chulo remained where he was and Breck felt his back muscles crawl. He turned slightly to keep the gunman in the corner of his eye.

"Malone!" Hecker said pleasantly. "I've been thinking about you, and here you are."

"I haven't forgotten you."

"I know. Red Hollings. He'll not bother you again."

"I don't expect him to," Breck said flatly.

A glint came into Hecker's eyes and vanished in a second. "I've been wanting to talk to you since you brought Red in. There's a table over in the corner that's private enough. Join me?"

He ordered bottle and glasses and, with a questioning look at Breck, walked to the table. Chulo Wyeth started to turn, but Jerry shook his head.

"Stay at the bar. Malone will feel better."

Chulo's heavy face pulled into a scowl, but he strode to the bar. Breck slowly walked to the table and sat down. Jerry poured drinks, handed a glass to Breck. "To your health, Malone."

"And yours."

Jerry grinned. "You're saying I'll need it. You're right. You know the kind of outfit I head up?"

"Killers, rustlers, hardcases—who doesn't know?"

"Exactly, Malone. Most of my boys are pretty fast with a gun."

"Meaning?"

"So are you. Red's supposed to be good, but you beat him."

"Are you praising me for shooting one of your men?"

Jerry's eyes twinkled as he looked at Breck. "I guess I am. Red had it coming. From now on in, he'll get his steaks in the usual way."

Breck said nothing, waiting. Hecker had more than this half apology on his mind, would not have bothered unless there were other, more important motives.

Jerry studied his drink, then looked up at Breck, his flecked eyes sharp and hard. "Red asked for trouble and got it. But it amounts to one of my bunch being shot and arrested, and the boys expect me to do something about it.

"If you get away with it, someone else will try. We don't give a damn if people don't like us, so long as they're too scared to do anything about it. Now it looks like you might."

Breck's jaw set. "I don't scare easy."

Jerry made a slight grimace. "Let's not talk about scaring off and riding out. You've got brains enough to know

43

where you stand. I hope that we can talk things over and come to a deal."

"A deal? Like throwing in with you?"

"You're all wrong for us, or any wild bunch. Give me credit for some brains, too. No, I'm thinking about your spread."

"The ranch!"

Jerry folded his hands on the table. "I reckon you know a man gets ahead in these parts if we let him. You could find out how you'll do, I suppose. On the other hand, you might plan to leave. In that case, I'd like to buy the Circle M."

Breck smiled his disbelief. "Why don't you just take over —if you can?"

"That wouldn't give me legal title. A horse, a cow, money —they belong to whoever can take them. But land is different. I'll pay the going price. You can leave with money in your pocket."

"Suppose I turn it down?"

"Do I have to tell you?" He stood up. Instantly Chulo Wyeth stepped from the bar. "Think it over and let me know."

"When?"

"You're not being forced to sell and run. Don't take too long, though. The boys won't like it, and neither will I."

He gave a slight bow and walked to the door, Chulo behind him. At the batwings, the big gunslinger looked back at Breck with dislike. He spat, hitched at his gun and walked out.

Breck slowly stood up. The three punchers and the bartender watched him with veiled curiosity, one of them with the ghost of a knowing smile. That smirk angered Breck, for it seemed a symbol of the way everyone's face would look if he pulled out, overawed and beaten, without a fight.

The next night he again had a sample of the fear and suspicion that gripped the San Alma country. Though he was expected, he was challenged as he rode toward the dark shadows of Matt Unger's ranch house. He instantly drew rein and sang out his name. Three armed men drifted up and a bull's-eye lantern flashed briefly on his face. He was passed.

By the time he had tied his horse at the rack and approached the dark house, his anger boiled again. Jerry Hecker had made these people tremble and skulk when they should stride freely, like men. Now Hecker had started on him.

44

Matt Unger peered out the door at Breck's knock and then threw it wide. "Come in, Breck!"

The spacious room was made bright and cheerful by several lamps. The furniture was heavy, handmade, built to supply masculine comfort.

Doc Vance, coat off and vest unbuttoned, stood by the big stone fireplace, a whiskey in his hand. He grinned at Breck and then spoke sharply. "Come alone?"

"Sure," Breck answered, puzzled.

Matt Unger introduced Breck to two other men. Both were of the same massive build, but one was a florid forty and the other a heavy sixty. The younger was Dan Lashlee, who owned a spread just west of the valley. Breck detected a slight nervousness in his hearty voice and wide gestures. The older man, Chad Sears, came from the southern part of the county, a rancher and grain dealer in the small town of Riata.

Matt turned Breck toward a third man, who stood up and extended his hand. "I figured you'd be in to see me, and was afraid of it."

John Dean would have been taken for a cowboy masquerading in a business suit instead of San Alma's banker. He had an angular, ruddy face that looked as though the winds of the ranges had swept it. His keen blue eyes seemed to have gazed on great distances rather than on ledgers, notes and mortgages. His handclasp was firm, brief and yet friendly.

Breck chuckled. "I still might visit you."

"Only as a friend. Not for a ranch loan."

"What's wrong with Circle M?" Breck asked sharply.

"Lack of beef—caused by Hecker's gang. I know it as well as you. You're not alone, either."

"Business later, John," Unger cut in. He walked to a small table and poured a drink, handing it to Breck. The conversation became general: weather, beef prices, gossip and news from Sears and Lashlee. Breck stood beside Doc Vance, puzzled.

There was no sign of cards or chips and the presence of Lashlee and Sears for an evening of cards did not seem reasonable. Unger spoke to them. They nodded, seemed to argue in low tones. Once Sears looked directly at Breck, then hastily away. He deliberately turned his back and said something. Unger nodded.

Doc Vance refilled his glass and spoke to Breck, his voice carrying. "What's left of Circle M?"

Breck shrugged. "Enough so a man might have a chance."

Dean spoke up. "Hard facts, or just wishes?"

"Facts, mostly, with a wish here and there. It won't be easy, but the herd could be built up."

"If you're left alone," Unger said.

"I'd be a fool to figure on that after what the Hecker gang did to Uncle Jim. Besides, Hecker just offered to buy the spread."

"What!"

"Said he wanted legal title and offered going price."

The men exchanged surprised and worried glances. Dean rubbed his hand along his jaw. "A smart move for Hecker. Can't run him off, and he could use it as headquarters."

Unger broke the short period of heavy silence. "Are you going to take his offer?"

"Matt, I know Uncle Jim wanted me to hang on to it and make it grow. But I think of the way San Alma was when I left—and what it is now. Looks like Hecker rules the country and owns the law and the court."

Doc Vance growled, "You don't know how much." He launched into a brief, sulfurous recital of outlaw depredations, most of which Breck already knew. He added the names of two men, gunned down by the outlaws, who had been Breck's friends in the old days. Breck's lips thinned in an angry line.

"San Alma," Doc Vance ended in angry sarcasm, "outlaw roost and haven! You breathe when they tell you or you don't breathe at all. They got themselves a judge and a sheriff. That's the sort of thing you figure on now, Breck."

Breck caught the covert, weighing glances of Unger and the two ranchers. Dean studied his folded hands.

Unger cleared his throat. "Breck, that's what we face, but you can go off and leave it. Nobody would blame you."

"Except me — and Uncle Jim, wherever he is. I'm turning Hecker down, and I'm staying."

Doc Vance glared at the younger man. "Then you'll have to do something about the Hecker bunch. Willing to?"

"There's me, Tip, and two riders. Four men. We'll do what we can. Circle M will be unhealthy for outlaws, at least until they bury us."

Doc spoke to the others. "Is that answer enough?"

Breck stepped forward. "This is sure as hell no poker game!"

Doc Vance nodded. "That's right, Breck. Might have been if we figured you were running out. You would never have known about anything else." Doc spoke with a quiet and deep sincerity. "Breck, after what I'm going to tell you, one word from you and all of us could be dead. I'm asking for no promise, just leaving it up to you."

He waited. Breck nodded. "Read it out."

"Over two years ago, Matt, me and John Dean wondered what in hell could be done about Jerry Hecker. He had to be stopped, but we didn't know how. The thing just started in talk, but it ended with us trying to do something. We talked to other people around the county, secretly. We're a kind of organization representing those who want real law and real peace in San Alma."

Dean spoke up. "About all we've done is gripe and then hope."

Unger strode angrily to the table. "What else could we do? Go up against Hecker's gundogs? Or Cantro's speed? And us just ordinary men!"

"Get your feathers down, Matt," Doc Vance said quietly. "Of course we can't. But we know we've got every decent citizen in the county behind us."

"Then why haven't you done something?" Breck demanded.

Unger cut in. "We've needed someone who's got guts and can use a gun. With a man like that, we'd have a leader and we could get all the support we need."

Dean looked at Breck. "You see, we're getting a chance to take over San Alma county. It won't come again for four more years and we have to grab it sure this time."

"Elections," Unger snapped. "For sheriff. As it stands, Cantro is certain to get it. No one has dared run against him."

"Afraid of an outlaw bullet," Doc Vance said. "Don't blame 'em, but it still means Jerry Hecker runs us, ruins us and does what he pleases with us."

Breck looked from one to the other, then at John Dean. "What are you driving at?"

"Cantro is Hecker's man and Hecker intends to keep it that way," Dean said. "Deadline for filing as candidate for sheriff comes up shortly. Anyone else who files is a sure mark for outlaw bullets."

"That figures," Breck agreed.

"But — if that man could keep himself alive until voting day, he would be elected. Point is, we've never found anyone to buck Hecker and Cantro, or who could live long enough to pin on Cantro's star. We think we have such a man now."

Dean steepled his hands and looked around at the others. Then his blue eyes rested on Breck. His voice was low, but the single word struck like the stunning blow of a bullet.

"You!"

47

Chapter VI

BRECK EXCLAIMED, "But I've been gone ten years! There must be at least a dozen men——"

"There's not one," Doc Vance cut in.

"Why do you think I can stand up to Cantro?"

"We know a few things that happened to you down along the border." Doc Vance filled his glass as he spoke. "And we can guess a lot more. You don't work down there very long without using a six-gun, now, do you?"

"Well. . .no."

"And you handled Red Hollings. Any way you look at it, you're the man we've needed."

Matt growled, "Jim Malone was robbed blind and it killed him. They'll do the same to you. You need help and we'll pitch in. But we ask you to help us."

Breck's sharp glance cut to Lashlee, then to Sears. The older man seemed to read his silent question. "Matt asked us to look you over. We've heard about you. Now we've seen you. You can count on us in our districts."

"But I can't wear the star!"

"Why not?" Doc Vance demanded.

"That's a full-time job for four years. I can't do justice to it and Circle M both."

Matt said dryly, "There's not much at Circle M Tip Johnson can't handle."

Dean held up his hand and the rest fell silent. "I don't think Breck should make up his mind tonight."

"I can't. I don't know what to figure on."

"You can figure on outlaws, one way or another. We're working out a plan, but a lot will depend on you."

"That's damn little to go on," Breck objected.

"I know, but think it over. Let us know in a week. Decide any way you want. We only ask that you keep tonight's meeting secret."

"I promise that."

"Good!" Dean looked at his watch and grinned at the others. "I've had enough poker for the night."

The meeting broke up. Lashlee and Sears rode out. Doc Vance took his leave after a final word to Breck. Unger closed the door after him and moved back into the room.

48

"Have another drink, Breck. Give Doc time to be on his way. We're careful we don't ride out in a bunch—just in case."

Shortly after, Breck mounted, neck-reined his horse and headed for home, his mind in turmoil. He still felt a shocked surprise at the offer and a sense of pleasure that old friends had so much confidence in him.

He considered the problem. Cantro could not continue as sheriff if the outlaws were to be driven out of the county. But Breck was not sure he could afford to give the time to the job—if he lived long enough to get it. Still, he faced a fight with the outlaws, with or without friends. He decided to consider everything tomorrow, a night's sleep away from the appeal of the men he had just left.

He touched spurs to his horse, aware that he was but a short distance from home. Then, faintly, over the drumming of the hoofs, he heard an alien sound. He drew rein and sat listening. It came again—the ragged, flat reports of gunfire ahead—and he saw a red glow against the sky.

Those shots and that glow could only come from the Circle M. He raked the spurs and the horse bolted forward. The glow looked brighter. He heard shots now, even over the drum of the hoofs.

He drew rein, listening. He heard more shots and placed the attackers between himself and the ranch. He drifted forward, gun now in his hand, eyes searching the night shadows.

He topped a small rise and, through a line of trees, saw flames enveloping a small storage shed, the flying sparks threatening the barn. He saw lances of gunfire among the trees and the answering fire from the bunkhouse and the main ranch building.

Breck drifted toward the trees. He knew that the sound of galloping hoofs would invite the concentrated fire of the outlaws. He moved in slowly, counting the sporadic lances of gun flame until he had each bushwhacker placed.

He drew rein and waited until he saw the gun flame lick from an outlaw's Colt. Breck slammed a shot just above it. He raked spurs and, with a screeching yell, swept toward the outlaws, gun roaring as his slugs sought out the hidden men.

The unexpected attack sent panic through the renegades. Shadowy figures jumped up and Breck's bullets sent one tumbling, made a second stagger. He caught the shape of horses and saw men swinging into saddle. Guns thundered and he heard the whine of bullets, but the outlaw fire was hurried. Breck raced off into the darkness, made a short turn and came charging in from another direction. At the

49

same moment, Tip, Chuck and Lew attacked, guns blazing.

The outlaws milled as Breck thundered out of the darkness and his bullets sought them. Tip and his men raced in from another direction.

The renegades broke, scattered, riding off in all directions. Breck drew rein and called to Tip as the thunder of the fleeing renegades faded and was gone. "The fire! It'll catch the barn!"

He raced to the well. As the hands came running up, Breck swiftly formed them into a bucket line. The four worked furiously but Breck wondered if fire would not complete what outlaw guns had started.

Twice the barn seemed about to catch fire, but each time the smoldering threat was beaten. At last there were only a few faint embers in the blackened pile of ash and charred studding that had once been the shed.

Breck wearily joined the others at the edge of the burned area. "What did we lose?" he asked Tip.

"A few tools, mostly. But if it had caught the barn. . . ."

Breck looked toward the trees. "Some of that bunch caught lead back there. We'd better take a look-see."

Breck and the men cautiously approached the trees, fanning out, guns ready. Tip sang out from the far end of the line. "Here's one!"

At the same moment, Breck saw a sprawling shape just ahead. He rolled the limp form over. "This one's dead. How about the one you found?"

"Dead." Tip looked at the lifeless renegade. "Hecker's bunch. He won't like this. He'll have to even the score or he won't be able to ramrod his bunch of wolves."

"I expect so. But maybe there's something we can do about it. We'd better deliver these two to San Alma come morning."

The bodies were carried to the barn and then they inspected the ranch house. Very little damage had been done and most of it could be patched up.

Tip told him about the attack. Chuck and Lew had just gone to the bunkhouse when the outlaws struck with no warning. One of them had set fire to the shed while the rest covered him. Tip believed the outlaws had planned to gun down the crew as they ran out to fight the flames.

Breck shook his head. "No, it was a scare. Hecker wanted to panic me into selling out."

"I'd say *they* got the scare and the worst of the deal."

Breck chuckled. "Tomorrow we'll see how Hecker likes the joke."

Early the next morning, the two dead outlaws were lashed

across lead horses. Breck and Tip rode out, the lead horses wih their burdens trotting behind them. On the outskirts of San Alma, Breck grimly checked his gun.

A horseman, coming toward them, drew rein, stared and then wheeled about and galloped toward the courthouse. Faces appeared at windows. Men stood in doorways or by the hitchracks, eying the limp bodies.

Breck and Tip came into the main business district. Breck saw people crowding store doorways and windows. He glanced at the tarp-covered bodies and headed into the sheriff's hitchrack.

He drew rein and, without dismounting, lifted his voice in a call that carried clearly down the street. "Cantro! Cantro!"

The office door opened and Cantro appeared. He looked at the bodies, at the onlookers several yards away, then sharply up at Breck. His thumbs were hooked into his gun belt, his right hand close to the holster. "What's all this about?"

"Is Jerry Hecker in town?"

"How should I know? Am I supposed to—"

"At the Cattleman's!" a man in the crowd sang out.

Breck smiled frostily and indicated the still forms on the horses. "I've got something to tell him and you ought to hear it, Cantro. Coming along?"

"More killing, Malone? I'll handle this."

"After I've seen Hecker. Anything against that?"

Cantro's nostrils flared, but he became aware of the townsmen who pressed closer now, emboldened by their curiosity. His black eyes darted to Breck's gun belt and to Tip, whose right hand hung easily just below his holster. "If you're planning trouble, I warn you—"

Breck unbuckled his gun belt, hung it on the saddlehorn. He signalled Tip to do the same, then faced the sheriff. "Satisfied?"

Without waiting for an answer, he gathered up the reins of the lead horses and walked across the street to the Cattleman. Cantro, after throwing a venomous look at the crowd, walked slowly after him.

Breck mounted the steps to the saloon porch. Just then, Jerry Hecker came out, Chulo Wyeth behind him. Hecker's coat was unbuttoned and the sun caught the bright cartridges in the gun belt he wore.

"Something wrong?" Chulo growled.

"Not yet," Hecker answered, a steel edge to his voice.

Breck's smile held grim humor. "Then I'm about to ruin your day."

51

Jerry's eyes dropped to Breck's waist, noted the absence of holster and gun. He saw the grim loads the horses carried. His eyes widened, flared in anger and then hooded as Breck turned to the animals.

Breck and Tip loosened the ropes that held the bodies, then flipped back the tarp and exposed the faces. Cantro and the townsmen could see the dead men as Breck spoke to Hecker, now on the edge of the saloon porch.

"Your boys, Jerry. They paid a gun call at my ranch last night."

Hecker spoke tightly. "What has this got to do with me?"

"Don't tell me you haven't heard about that little party!" Breck indicated the bodies again. "Here they are, returned to you—a whole lot worse for wear." His voice grew grim, harsh and lifted clearly. "Consider this a fair warning, you and your sheriff. I'll defend my property, if no one else will."

Cantro's face paled. Chulo Wyeth's hand darted to his gun. Hecker's fingers wrapped about the big man's wrist, forcing the Colt deep in the holster.

"No! He wears no gun. There's always another time."

"When? Tonight?" Breck demanded.

Hecker fought for control and finally achieved it. He walked calmly down the steps and looked at the dead outlaws. "If these two attacked your place, they did it on their own. I know nothing about it."

Breck smiled thinly. "Neither do they—now. Better bury them."

Hecker's voice was sharp, steel-edged. "I'm blamed for everything, including this. I was in town last night."

"I figured you'd be clear, with witnesses to prove it."

A ring of white appeared around Hecker's lips. "I'll let that pass. But remember, these two boys have friends. They're bound to hear of it."

"Tell them Circle M is ready if they want to even the score, or if you want to do your own killing." Breck turned to find Cantro facing him, black eyes glittering. Breck's brows shot up. "Since when did the law back a gunhawk's threats? Or does San Alma have a special kind of law?"

Cantro's hand jerked to his gun and then he realized, again, that Breck was unarmed. He turned, shoulders rigid, and walked back to his office. Breck and Tip picked up the reins of the packhorses. Breck met Hecker's murderous eyes, held them a moment, and then turned away.

In a tense silence, he and Tip mounted and rode slowly down the street. Hecker stood without moving, every angle of his body showing anger. The townsmen watched.

Breck was near the bank when he suddenly dismounted

and pitched his reins to Tip. "I've got some business with John Dean."

"You ain't any kind of a risk for a loan—now."

Breck grinned. "I can always ask, I reckon."

He walked into the bank and asked to see Dean. In a moment Breck was ushered into an inner office.

John Dean regarded him from across a desk, a twinkle in his eyes. "I hear you've just had a meeting with our leading citizen."

"We swapped ideas and I gave him a present."

"Is that why you're here?"

"In a way. Any chance of seeing the boys at Matt's place?"

Dean's eyes glowed. "Say, two nights from now? Our friends outside the Valley ought to be there then."

"That'll be fine. See you then."

Breck walked out. Dean called after him. "Can't even think of a loan now, Malone."

Two nights later, he faced the group in Matt Unger's big room. Dean sat in the chair and Doc Vance rocked back and forth, shaggy brows knitted as he looked at Breck. Lashlee and Sears waited expectantly. Matt Unger looked at Breck. "You called this meeting. You've made up your mind?"

"I have." Breck took a breath. "Gents, I'll try for sheriff. How do we go about it?"

Chapter VII

"GLORY BE!" Matt whooped. "You don't know what this means to us."

"I do!" Doc Vance snorted. "Breck, I don't want you to take this job without knowing exactly what you face."

"I know, Doc. It's fight or run. But I might as well fight for more than Circle M while I'm at it."

"That's good enough for me," Lashlee said flatly.

Doc grunted. "How are you going to feel when the chips are down? Breck has put us beyond the talking stage. Every one of us will go down in Hecker's book. You can expect raids, rustling and bushwhack, or just plain murder. You have to be ready for it. Are you?"

Doc Vance poured himself a whiskey. "Since I asked the question, I ought to answer it first. I'm not much of a man if I'm not willing to back up what I believe is right. I'm a sinful, drinking old goat who's been overdue in hell ten years anyhow, but I want to do one *big* decent thing in my life."

Dean chuckled dryly. "I feel the same way. Count me in."

Matt nodded vigorously. "I'll ride this trail."

"And me," Sears boomed.

"Count me," Lashlee echoed.

Doc looked around at them. "Then we'll back Breck to the limit and go down with him if that happens? Your word for it?"

The pledge was made. Doc straightened, as though a big weight had been lifted from his shoulders, and looked at the banker.

"John, Breck asked how we go about it. You answer him."

Dean studied his fingertips for a long moment. "Gentlemen, let's sit down and work this out among us."

It was a council of war, and they all knew it. The hours passed; ideas were presented, accepted, rejected or amended. At last, Dean leaned back, weary as the rest, but satisfied.

"All right, we're agreed then. Lashlee, you'll see the folks down your way and you'll do the same around Riata, Sears. Matt, can you take care of the Valley? Doc and I will handle the town."

"And me?" Breck asked.

"You stick close to the ranch and keep quiet until the time comes to file for office."

"But at least I could help Matt round up the Valley folks!"

"No," Doc Vance said flatly. "Any risk we take now will be nothing to yours during the two months from filing to election day. You'll be the target for every outlaw, gunslinger and bushwhacker. There won't be a trick, ambush, raid or rustling that Hecker won't use against you."

Dean stood up. "There's nothing more we can do right now. Each knows his job. We'll keep one another posted."

"And me?" Breck asked.

"Run Circle M. If you come in for supplies, buy Doc a drink. That way, you'll know how things are going."

Dean looked around at the men. "Well, gentlemen, this is what we've been hoping for. Work like hell and pray for luck."

In the week that followed, Breck remained close to Circle M. Now that he had definitely decided to stay, Breck took hold with a new vigor. Corrals, fences, buildings and equipment were checked, replaced and repaired. He constantly watched the herd and rode the range, seeking any sign of the outlaws. It was an intensely busy period. Even at the end of the first week, there were visible signs of new vitality at Circle M. Breck also felt a change in himself. Now he had a purpose and goal, a place that was his where he could sink roots—depending, of course, on the success of the venture to which he was committed.

The lack of any sign of the outlaws worried Breck. Each night he felt that darkness would bring the Hecker bunch, but morning would dawn peacefully. This was not like Hecker. Retaliation had to come or he would lose control of his men. Toward the end of the week, Breck wondered if Hecker deliberately stayed away to build up tension and nervousness before he actually struck.

Breck often caught himself watching the road and wondering what could be happening. Would the ranchers and townsmen rally, or was everyone too cowed by outlaw rule? Breck tried to hide his impatience and his worry, for he felt that the less known about this the better, especially when nothing definite had developed.

On Saturday morning, Breck walked out to the corral where Tip and the men were having a last cigarette before roping their horses. Breck squinted up at the sun and then looked eastward where the Thunders and Granadas merged in the distance. The world out there beckoned him.

"Chuck, you and Lew head back in as soon as you can.

55

We've worked dog-hard all week. I figure we're due for a day in town."

Just before noon, Breck and his crew, dressed in their best, headed for San Alma. They set a fast pace and, as they left Circle M range, Breck felt all the excitement of a school-boy playing hookey.

At the edge of San Alma, Breck drew rein and, as the others pulled in beside him, he held out his hand. "Let me have your gun belts."

"Now wait, Breck!" Tip exclaimed.

"I can't afford any funerals. Shuck your guns. That's an order."

They reluctantly unbuckled their belts and handed them over, one by one. Breck draped them on the saddlehorn and then added his own.

"Now they won't pull Colts on you. I figure you can handle yourselves in any other kind of fight. Stay away from the Cattleman. Other than that, do as you please. I'll arrange rooms for us at the hotel. Head there if you get sleepy or drunk. Have yourselves a hooraw."

They cantered down the main street and circled the courthouse. Chuck, Lew and Tip headed directly for the Thunder. Breck stopped at the hotel. When he emerged, the gun belts were in each man's room. Breck looked toward the Cattleman.

There was no one on the porch and only two horses at the hitchrack. He felt a mild surprise that the wild bunch was not more in evidence. However, he knew they would show up before sundown. Saturday night in town was tra-ditional with everyone—rancher as well as outlaw.

He went to Dane's store. The place was crowded with people from the outlying ranches making their weekly pur-chases. Frank Dane was helping two men at the rear of the store. The clerk measured calico from a thick bolt for a rancher's wife. Alice worked her way down the crowded aisle to him.

"And where have you been, Mr. Malone?"

"At the ranch."

"Day and night, all the time? I'm about to be very angry with you."

"Why?"

"You've completely disregarded me."

"Not my fault. Partly because I've been busy and...well, I've been gone a long time and things change. I don't want to...step on someone's toes."

She looked at him in surprise. "Now whatever gave you that idea?" Her lips set in exasperated anger. "You can

56

change your mind right this minute, Breck Malone. I'm not pledged to anyone."

His face lighted. "Now I'm glad to hear that!"

"Are you?" She smiled suddenly. "Then I'll expect you for supper tonight, without fail."

He blinked. "But I didn't expect—"

"Without fail!"

She swept away before he could reply. He watched her, grinning, and then worked his way to the door and out onto the street.

He watched the usual Saturday stream of buggies, wagons, horses and people. He worked his way to the Thunder. The bar was lined with ranchers and their riders and Breck wondered if these were men whom Unger or Dean had contacted. A hand slapped his shoulder and he turned to face Doc Vance.

"Breck Malone! Thought you'd dropped in a hole somewhere. How about a drink?"

Doc indicated a table against a far wall. They sat down and Doc's voice dropped to a serious note. "None of the Hecker bunch around, but you can never tell who might take word to 'em."

"Where are they?" Breck asked.

"Don't know. Sometimes they don't show up, but you can depend on it, they'll be back."

"I haven't heard from you or Matt."

"Too busy, but everything goes well."

Doc Vance looked about the room. "Not a one I've talked to isn't ready to do something about Hecker. Not right out in the open yet, but that'll come."

"Then we can count on—"

"A lot more than we figured, leastways in town."

"How about Matt and the others?"

"Matt says he's getting support. All we needed was someone like you."

"Do they know about me?"

"Not by name yet. But the fact that someone's willing to run for sheriff is enough right now. We'll hold a meeting later on. Some safe place. You'll get word."

Doc Vance stood up and his voice lifted. "Malone, we'll swap lies again sometime. Right now, I've got some patients to see."

He waved his hand and left. Breck sat at the table, considering his half-filled whiskey glass. He tried to keep the elation out of his eyes and face as he reviewed the news Doc had brought. It confirmed his feeling that if the decent people of San Alma banded together...

He sensed a presence and his head jerked up. Roy Cantro stood across the table.

"Sheriff?"

Cantro indicated the table. "I'd like to join you."

"You surprise me, Cantro."

The sheriff took Doc Vance's seat. "I know. I was mad the last time we met. You were acting damn highhanded and had brought in two dead men. Malone, you explained nothing. It was after you left I began to get the story."

"From Hecker?"

"He didn't know, said he had no part in it. I told him I'd find out, check both your stories."

"That's easy. My crew's in town."

Cantro's jaw was outthrust. "I'll talk to them."

"And then what?"

"I'll find out who took part in the raid. When I do . . ."

Cantro talks big, Breck thought, promises much and delivers little. Hecker had already said he knew nothing of the raid. It would end there, though Cantro wanted people to think he tried to do something about it.

Cantro frowned. "But there's something else. Since you've come back, there's been nothing but trouble."

"My fault?"

"Maybe not, but still trouble. I sure wish you'd think real hard before you decide to stay on at Circle M. You've made enemies. Anything can happen. Jerry Hecker's no man to accuse like you did. I don't know what he'll do."

"But what will *you* do?"

"Me?"

"About Hecker. He's outlaw and you're sheriff."

Cantro said shortly, "If they've done anything wrong—"

"They have. I know it."

"I arrested Red Hollings, Malone. That was on direct evidence."

"He was released."

"There's no way of knowing what will happen at a trial."

"That sure makes it handy for Hecker," Breck said quietly.

Cantro stood up, leaned across the table. "I didn't come to argue but to warn you to be careful."

"Thanks," Breck said dryly.

Cantro spoke tightly. "Malone, I'll warn you again. You sure need it. After all, a lawman can't be everywhere at once."

He turned on his heel and walked away.

Later, Breck went to the Dane home, not too certain that

the evening would be pleasant. He was fairly sure Cantro would be there.

Alice, warm and gay as ever, made him welcome. Frank Dane shook hands and said he was glad to see Breck in a tone that proved he wasn't. Breck wondered at the barren welcome. Cantro was not present and a chance remark of Dane's explained his absence; on Saturday nights he patrolled the main portion of town.

"A good sheriff," Dane said. "Not much happens that he's not right on the spot to take care of."

Breck was glad that Alice called supper at that moment. Dane had little to say during the meal. Twice, Breck caught Alice looking at her father with a puzzled expression and she tried time and again to pull him into the conversation. She finally gave up and confined her easy, light talk to Breck.

After the meal, Dane excused himself to check the store. He brushed Alice's cheek with his lips, looked sharply at Breck and seemed on the verge of saying something. Instead, he clapped his hat on his head and left.

Afterwards, as Breck helped Alice in the kitchen, she asked about the ranch. He told her of his decision to stay on.

Alice looked worried. "Will Jerry Hecker leave you alone? I heard what happened the other day."

"Probably not. But he knows Circle M won't be healthy."

"That can work both ways," she warned.

He didn't answer, but his silence told her of his determination.

By the time they came out of the kitchen, Frank Dane had returned and was at the table in the front room, going over the store's accounts for the day. Alice led the way to the front porch and Breck saw Dane look up, bite his lip and then return to his figures.

Breck sat beside her on the swing. The light from the window cast a soft, golden glow over Alice, making her look almost ethereal. Dane's shadow momentarily cut the light.

"Your father's changed," Breck said suddenly.

"You've noticed?"

"Ten years ago he was real friendly to me. Now..."

Alice sighed. "He has changed. He used to be fun, but lately he pulls away, even from me."

Suddenly Breck chuckled and Alice looked inquiringly at him. "Remember the time Uncle Jim brought me here and I managed to knock that big lamp off the table? Frank talked a blue streak then!"

She laughed. "You could be the most awkward man I ever saw. Why, I recall . . ."

It took them into the past. Uncle Jim and all the warmth of the old days seemed to come alive.

"And the time I kissed you," she said. "Right in front of Dad and Uncle Jim. I thought you'd run right through the door, you were so scared."

"Embarrassed," Breck corrected. "You did that deliberately. You were an awful pest."

"I was in love with you then."

Their smiles remained, but there was something more. Slowly Alice lifted her hand to his cheek, touched it. Her eyes widened and she spoke in an awed voice.

"Breck? Breck . . . I still am."

Chapter VIII

BRECK DID NOT MOVE. He tried to speak but couldn't find the words. Suddenly he had her close in his arms, kissing her. Everything disappeared except the feel of her lips.

Frank Dane's angry roar came like a thunderclap. "Alice! Malone! What goes on out here?"

They sprang apart and jumped up. Her face was radiant as she started to speak. Dane's harsh voice lashed at her. "In my own home! With my own daughter!"

"But, Dad, I—"

"Get inside!"

Breck protested. "Frank—"

Dane savagely turned on him. "Get out of here! I don't want to see you again."

"Father!"

"Get inside!"

"I'll not do it. You have no right—"

"I have every right!" Dane glared at Breck. "Do you leave or do I call the sheriff?"

Breck tried to hold his voice level. "Frank, I tried to tell you that Alice and me—"

"Get out!"

The old man lifted his fist, his angry face clearly etched by the lamplight from the window. Breck realized his anger covered something close to fear. He frowned, trying to understand. Dane took a lunging step toward him. Alice caught his arm.

"Dad! Please!" She threw an appealing look at Breck. "Maybe you'd better."

Breck, jaw set, strode off the porch and down the walk. He threw a glance over his shoulder. Dane stood at the top of the porch steps, body rigid. Alice still held him. Breck walked blindly away. He seethed with anger but, under it, was a questioning of the old man's fear that had showed so plainly for a moment.

The side street paralleled the main thoroughfare, ending abruptly at the edge of the dark, rolling grassland beyond the town. Breck did not stop until he was at least a hundred yards beyond the last house. Then he turned about and looked back.

He could hardly see the low shadow of the houses or the higher black shapes of the trees. He took several deep breaths and his sense of balance returned.

He understood how Frank resented finding his daughter being kissed, but a man should have a chance to explain. He felt that Dane's anger was false and that fear was the real cause of the outburst.

Then Breck thought of the strange and wonderful thing that had happened. Had life forced him on a wandering, restless search for something he could not define only to find it, ten years later, right back where he had started? Why hadn't he recognized Alice as the woman for him long before?

He wondered at his blindness, but knew all this could never have come about without his having matured. Now he had a double reason for staying on, for making San Alma safe.

He looked northward toward the Thunders. Up there was the true threat to anything he and Alice might plan—Jerry Hecker. Once that was gone...

He suddenly recalled Cantro's holding Alice's hand, assured and smiling as he hinted that he had a very definite claim. Cantro could cause real trouble. So Breck had two men to fight—Alice's father and a sheriff who was a deadly man with a gun.

Breck thoughtfully started back the way he had come. He could not avoid trouble with Cantro in any case. His promise to Matt Unger, John Dean and the others made a showdown inevitable. He might as well fight for girl *and* badge.

He cut over to the main street, saw the lights of the two saloons and went into the Thunder.

He blinked against the bright light from the hanging lamps for a moment and heard the noise of a dozen conversations, the clink of poker chips, a burst of laughter. His eyes adjusted and he looked over the crowd. Tip came toward him.

Breck smiled. "I came for a last drink before I go to bed."

"Join us. We're just getting used to the firewater."

The leathery-faced foreman pushed into the crowd at the bar and found Breck a place beside Chuck, who grinned and lifted his glass. Lew shoved back his hat and frowned in marked discontent.

"There ain't been no real excitement, Breck."

Breck signalled a drink from perspiring Tom Wheeler behind the bar. "Feel glad our friends haven't showed up."

"That's what I told 'em," Tip growled. "But these two get cocky with a few drinks."

"I'll remember that," Breck said soberly.

He tossed his drink and half listened to the buzz of talk. He bought another round for Tip and the men. Then Cantro appeared at the bar, grinning and affable as he looked around. He saw Breck and moved up beside him. "No hard feelings about this afternoon?"

"Why does that matter?"

Cantro's dark eyes lost their hardness and seemed, for the moment, to look into the past. "Maybe because I keep remembering that you know about Tres Cruces."

"I was there long after you left."

"But you know about me. You know what it was like—and what I was like. But, hell! A man can't live in the past."

"No," Breck said slowly, "but sometimes he should remember." Cantro studied Breck, apparently on the edge of decision. Then the moment passed. He pushed away from the bar with a flashing, hard smile. "Well, this is San Alma, and a damned quiet night."

Tom Wheeler glanced hurriedly up from his bottles and glasses. "Making another patrol, Sheriff?"

"Waste of time, peaceful as things are." He chuckled. "Tell the boys not to raise hell, Tom. I want to hang up my badge until morning."

He nodded to Breck, pushed through the crowd and was gone.

Breck had the feeling he had come close to understanding Cantro. It was something about Tres Cruces and San Alma. Cantro had been one kind of lawman there, a totally different kind here. Why? Cantro had been at the point of explanation, and then the moment had gone. What had changed him? He dismissed the matter when Tip suggested another round.

Breck found relaxation in the press of men, the idle talk, the pleasant glow from the drinks. He idled away nearly an hour there, then walked to the hotel and climbed the stairs to his room. He lit the lamp, pulled the blind and sat down on the edge of the bed.

He smiled softly when he thought of Alice. Then he frowned as he wondered if Frank Dane had finally simmered down enough so she could explain.

He stood up, stretched and unbuttoned his shirt. Feet pounded up the stairs and strode along the corridor. They stopped, and a fist pounded on his door. Breck whipped about, startled. His eyes shot to his gun and belt on the dresser, but he strode to the door and flung it open.

63

Cantro stood in the hall. His face was drawn and harsh. His eyes blazed. Before Breck could move, Cantro pushed inside, closed the door behind him and leaned against it. He glared at Breck, unable to speak for a moment.

"You sneaking son!" he finally choked out.

Breck jerked as though Cantro had hit him. "Sneaking?"

"I've just come from the Danes."

"Oh . . . you saw Alice."

"She wouldn't come out. I talked to Frank. He told me what happened. I'll not let you get away with it, Malone. You stay away from her."

"I think that's up to Alice."

"She's *my* girl. Get that straight and don't forget it. I'll have no one fooling around. You stay away from her, understand? If you don't—"

"Cantro!" Breck faced him squarely, fists doubled at his side. He took a deep breath to relieve his tension. His voice leveled. "Are you engaged to her?"

Cantro started to nod, then caught himself. His jaw set. "We will be, soon."

"If you have your way. Has Alice agreed to marry you?"

Cantro's nostrils flared. "Not in so many words, but—"

"Then you have no claim."

"I'm warning you to stay away from her."

Breck smiled tightly. "Frank Dane ordered me out of the house. That's his right and I respect it. But Alice and I can make up our own minds. Neither Frank nor you can stop that."

"By God—"

"You're warning me," Breck finished for him, words clipped. "I'm warning you. I'll see Alice Dane every chance I get. And something else. She's going to be my wife, if I can persuade her."

Cantro stood transfixed for a long moment. Then he exploded so suddenly that Breck was caught off balance. Cantro's fist crashed against Breck's jaw, slamming him backward, and he fought to get his balance. Cantro bored in, fighting with such furious blind anger that, for the moment, Breck could only try to protect himself.

Fists caught him in the ribs, bounced off his arms, struck the top of his head. He was driven back, slammed against the wall with such force that the whole building shook. Cantro was on him, pummelling, fingers clawing for his eyes, then doubling into fists and smashing at him.

The wall gave Breck the support he had so desperately sought. He brought up his fist in a piston blow that caught Cantro in the chest. The man staggered, mouth flying open.

Breck threw a punch that caught him on the cheek and slammed the man back against the washstand. The stand tipped over and the china bowl and pitcher, filled with water, crashed to the floor.

Cantro clutched wildly at the wall, hung there a moment and then, with a savage roar, propelled himself forward, head lowered, taloned hands reaching for Breck. Breck threw a looping blow that caught Cantro on the forehead. It half straightened him and Breck stepped in and slammed his fist in a glancing blow against the man's jaw.

Cantro fell back against the wall beside the door. His eyes were wild and all reason had left him. His hand slashed to his holster and the light glinted on the heavy Colt as it blurred upward.

Just then, the door burst open and men surged inside. Breck tensed himself for the smash of the bullet, coming up on the balls of his feet ready for a desperate, hopeless rush to beat the slug. Cantro's gun leveled, his thumb dogging back the hammer. He remained frozen in that position as the frightened, excited men lunged into the room.

Breck's breath eased out in a loud sigh and he settled back on his heels. Cantro's eyes went to the men, then back to Breck. His lips pulled back over his teeth in a look of disappointed rage that he swiftly erased from his face.

"Sheriff! What's wrong?" the hotel clerk demanded.

Cantro kept his gun leveled on Breck. He wiped his hand across his mouth, smearing a trickle of blood. "I came up here to arrest Malone. He resisted."

"You're a liar, Cantro," Breck said. The man's finger whitened against the trigger. Cantro ached for the excuse to shoot. "But make your arrest."

Cantro glared at him but he sensed that he had been forced to bring a charge against Breck. He made a motion toward the door with the gun muzzle. "I got a cell waiting for you."

"What charge?"

Cantro looked trapped, knowing that he must have a reason for arrest or admit he had drawn a gun on an unarmed man in a private fight. He glared, boiling with barely restrained anger. "Disturbing the peace."

"I can prove where I was every minute of the time. My gun's over there, unfired. I've not even had it on. I—"

"You can tell it to the judge," Cantro snapped.

Breck saw Tip craning to see over the heads of the others and he answered Cantro but spoke directly to Tip. "So I can. Maybe as quick as Red Hollings if someone can get the judge."

"I'll get him," Cantro sneered and again motioned toward the door.

As Breck slowly walked out ahead of Cantro and his drawn gun, he caught Tip's eyes and gave a slight sign. He strode on down the stairs and out into the street. Tip headed toward the Thunder.

A few moments later, Cantro slammed the cell door and locked it while Breck sat down on the bunk, unconcerned. Cantro glared at him through the bars. Breck looked up. "Think you can make this stick?"

Cantro strode down the short corridor. Breck heard the slam of the heavy door. He was alone, behind the barred window. Only then did he slump back against the wall. He had been close to death, for Cantro would have shot to kill if the men hadn't rushed in.

The building itself was silent, but Breck listened for the first indication of Cantro's return, perhaps with murder on his mind. But he felt that with each passing minute, danger lessened. He wondered if Tip had caught his hint to find Judge Tracy.

Suddenly Breck straightened. Sounds from the street indicated that men strode toward the jail. He could hear the lift of their angry voices. Breck stood up, tense. Had Tip worked up some sort of a mob instead of getting the drunken judge? Jail break—Cantro's one perfect excuse—was the last thing Breck wanted.

Now Breck could hear the angry rise and fall of voices from beyond the closed corridor door. He grasped the bars, trying to make out words and phrases from the growling mumble. The door banged open. Cantro came striding down the hall as Tip's voice lifted in warning. Breck stepped back as the sheriff came to the door. Cantro, his face a mixture of emotions, inserted the key in the lock, his hand trembling. He swung the door wide.

"Outside." He stepped back and his hand touched his holstered gun. "Judge Tracy will see you—in there."

Breck moved slowly out into the corridor and could see down its length into the office. It was crowded with men, among them Doc Vance, Tip and some townsmen, all grim and waiting.

Cantro followed a few steps behind Breck as he walked into the office. He saw Judge Tracy, slack-jawed with drink and fright. Tracy's eyes cut to Tip, then the others. He pulled himself together as Cantro appeared in the doorway.

"Sheriff, I believe Mr. Malone is charged with a misdemeanor only. Disturbing the peace." He could not completely hide the slight quaver in his rounded, sonorous tones.

He managed a smile and waved his hand toward the grim men. "These good citizens have persuaded—"

"Now that's a good word, Judge," Tip said dryly.

Tracy flushed and grabbed his dignity once more. "I feel a man of Mr. Malone's standing should not suffer the indignity of jail on such a minor matter. Please state your charge, Sheriff, and we shall dispose of this case."

Cantro stood quite still, knowing he had made a fool of himself but seeking some means of saving his ego. Breck saw that something else surprised Cantro. He had not believed that angry citizens would dare challenge any of his acts.

Doc Vance moved restlessly. "Speak your piece, Cantro, and produce your evidence. I might add all of us are witnesses *for* Malone."

Cantro's voice was a low growl. "No charges." His voice became muffled. "Maybe I was mistaken."

Tracy blinked and threw a sidelong glance at Doc Vance. "In that case, there's nothing to do but release Mr. Malone. So ordered."

He slapped his hand on the desk and, as Tip and Doc Vance surged toward Breck, sidled through the crowd and out the door. Breck grinned at Tip, who jerked his thumb toward Doc Vance. "He got the judge—and the crowd."

The foreman looked steadily at Cantro. "Seems like a lot of folks don't like highhanded sheriffs."

Cantro angrily turned on his heel. Breck's sharp voice checked him. "Cantro!" The sheriff turned. "Everything between us still stands."

"I warned you."

"So you did—and that stands, too. But next time there's a personal argument, don't pull a law badge."

Breck left Cantro seething, his anger directed as much against himself as against Breck.

Chapter IX

A WEEK LATER, lamplight glowed from behind the drawn curtains of a small cottage on the north edge of town. A man kept watch on the road. In the rear, four saddled horses stood ground-tied, heads drooping, waiting the coming of their riders.

In the parlor, Hallie Yates served whiskey and, avoiding Chulo Wyeth's admiring gaze, walked to a sofa and sat down, her dark beauty softened by the glow of the ornate table lamp.

Roy Cantro sat in a big chair and sipped his drink, apparently at ease. But Hallie saw the signs that she had long ago learned. She knew his smile went no deeper than the muscles that moved the lips.

Jerry Hecker sat in the chair that Roy normally used, looking little like an outlaw. Only the gun belt beneath his flawlessly cut black coat suggested violence. His round face was replete with good humor and his flecked eyes danced as he spoke of the past week.

"Things went very well with us, Roy, except for Snake Redfern. Had an accident while we were on the trip. A forty-four slug is pretty final."

Cantro took another hasty swallow and looked to Hallie for a refill. "You must have been pretty busy."

Hecker's smile acquired an edge. "There was a lot of business transacted. Means little to you, Roy."

"Of course," Cantro said shortly.

Hecker sipped his drink and placed his empty glass on the table. Hallie started to get up, but he signalled her to sit still.

"What makes a man lose his head?" he asked softly.

Cantro started. "What?"

"What makes a man lose his head—like you did with Breck Malone?"

Cantro sat quite still. Hecker's eyes were hard and direct now. Hallie suddenly saw the implacable deadliness in the man, the ruthless killer, and she knew the secret of his rule over men like Chulo Wyeth.

"You made a fool of yourself, Roy."

"Now look here! No one calls me a fool!"

Cantro sat bolt upright. Chulo Wyeth stood quite still,

waiting for a slight signal from the dapper man in the chair. Hallie, frightened, held her breath.

"Are you saying I can't, or that you'll do something about it?" Hecker's lips moved in a small, mirthless smile. "Why, Roy, you just go right ahead!"

Hallie came to her feet. Fear almost choked her. Cantro's hands gripped the ends of the chair arms, his face gaunt and tight, his eyes a metallic glitter. In a second, he would explode. Hallie had seen it before.

She hurried between him and Hecker, composing herself. She picked up the empty glasses.

"Now don't ruin good whiskey with bad tempers," she said lightly. "I pay too much for it."

For a second, Cantro remained frozen. Then he leaned back as his fingers loosened their tight grip. Hecker gave her an up-slanting look and she read approval in his flecked eyes.

She moved swiftly, wanting to keep attention on herself until the anger in both men subsided. She looked at Chulo and the empty glass in his left hand. He gave it to her, his eyes touching the V of her dress and then up, his thoughts so naked that she hastily turned away.

Soon she returned to her chair and the men sipped the liquor. The electrical tension in the room had vanished. Hecker's voice lost its edge. "This business about Malone. I heard it one way. Maybe you tell it another."

Cantro's hand rubbed the chair arm again. His lips flattened and then, with an imperceptible shrug, he told what had happened in brief, sharp words. It was the first time Hallie had heard the whole story. She watched Cantro, her face calm, but mixed emotions moving inside her.

"He's been trouble since he came," Cantro finished. "When I found out what he had done, I plain got mad."

Hecker sucked in his cheeks. "I can understand that. You can pick a fight with Malone anytime you want to and any way you want to."

"By God—"

"But carry it through. I don't say a fight is real smart right at this time, but if one comes, don't back down.

"People have to be afraid of you, Roy. If they can't buck you, it's damned certain they won't buck me, because I keep 'em more afraid of me than of you. Once they've got you on the run, they'll get ideas about me and my boys. I wouldn't like that one little bit."

"You're talking two ways, Jerry," Cantro said. "You're saying I'd better hunt him up and have it out. But you're also saying you don't think I should."

"In a way, I am. He *has* been trouble from the time he showed up. There was Red Hollings."

"How about those other two?"

Hecker grimaced angrily. "I made an offer to Malone for Circle M. I figured maybe a quick raid would make him sell out. But the boys had to show how damn good they were and make a real fight of it. So I lost two good men."

"One thing's sure, Jerry. If Malone stays on, you're going to have to handle him personally."

"I don't want to do that, yet."

Chulo spoke up eagerly. "What's wrong with me?"

"Everything!" Hecker snapped and Chulo subsided with a scowl. Hecker looked thoughtfully at the far wall, eyes narrowed. "We'd best let things drift along until after the election to make sure there's no chance of any upset."

"No one's going to file against me!"

"Let's make doubly certain and not have any more trouble."

"Now I'm to leave him alone?" Cantro asked sharply.

"That's right. Strictly alone."

"What if he fools around the Danes'?"

Hecker stood up and reached for his derby. He looked down at Cantro. "After election, we'll handle Breck Malone. But until then, forget him. Forget Alice Dane if you have to. That's an order."

Cantro stood up, face tight again. "And I don't like it."

Hecker's right hand hung close to the gun just beneath his coat. "Roy, in public I talk nice and soft about you, even take your orders just to make things look right." His eyes grew cold. "But don't forget for one minute who ramrods this town, this gang—and you. Sheriffs have ended in Boothill before, and it can happen again. That's a promise."

Hallie stood poised to throw herself between them. Chulo waited, eyes cutting from one man to the other, as if wondering which would make the first move for his gun. Except for the heavy rise and fall of Cantro's chest, neither seemed to move. Their eyes locked.

Then Cantro's slid away. He moistened his lips. "I'll stay out of his way."

His voice was muffled, shaken. Hecker studied him a second and then turned to Hallie, smiling as though nothing untoward had happened. "My thanks for the supper, the whiskey and the company. I hope to enjoy them all again, soon."

She caught her voice. "You're always welcome."

"I like to hear that. Chulo, we've got a long ride."

At the door, Hecker smiled at her again and then went out. Chulo stood there a second, muddy eyes on Cantro, and then gave her a murky look before he walked out, banging the door.

Hallie watched Cantro, but he seemed to be listening to the faint sounds from outside. She heard a brief, rolling beat of hoofs, and then silence. Cantro's head slowly swiveled and his black eyes blazed at her.

"Why do I take that?" he asked through set teeth.

"I'll get you a drink."

He dropped heavily into the chair. She brought him the drink and he gulped it down without looking at her, then savagely threw the empty glass across the room. It smashed against the wall and broke in a thousand fragments.

"An owlhooter! A ridgerunner! And I let him talk to *me* —Roy Cantro—that way!"

She sat down with a sigh. "You knew something like this would happen when you made your deal."

"But am I his flunky?"

"You sold yourself to him long ago, Roy. I never knew why, really why."

His face paled and she thought he would strike her. He lifted the cloth of his shirt so he could look at the badge. His lips moved in a grimace of distaste.

"What do you think of San Alma?" he asked abruptly.

"Why—just another town. What difference does it make where I sew a dress—and keep out of sight?"

He ignored the bitter note. "It's a town with no guts."

"Aren't they all?"

"But they back their sheriff!" He twisted around to face her. "You know what it was like in Tres Cruces. Sure, I was the one who had to handle the guns, but the whole town was behind me. I told a man to get out, he got out. Then I came here.

"Jip Terry used to tell me that San Alma was going to hell. It cared more about a dollar than law and order. He had his troubles, but he was about through and so they didn't push him."

He flung himself out of the chair. "The wild bunch came after I took the badge, and then I damned soon found out what I could expect of San Alma!"

"You take it too hard."

He wheeled on her. "Why shouldn't I? I used to be proud of this star—and proud of myself." His voice thickened with sarcasm. "That is, everywhere but in San Alma. I rode renegades out of town and what happened? They had money to spend, so the merchants said I drove off business. I tried to tell them I drove off gunplay, murder and robbery."

He smashed his fist into his palm. "Oh, I must uphold the

law, all right! But I must first make sure the gent with notches on his gun doesn't have money in his pockets!" He swung on her. "Remember the time they said I was too fast with a gun—using it first and asking questions after? What else do you do when you see a killer?"

He turned to the table and poured another slug of whiskey. "I finally knew San Alma didn't deserve any law. I should have left, but there wasn't any town looking for a sheriff or marshal then."

Cantro tossed the drink. "So Jerry Hecker came. He saw how it was. He knew how I felt. It was what he wanted. My God! how he pussyfooted around until he was sure I'd listen."

He faced her again. "So I gave this town exactly what it deserved. Now everyone's happy—Jerry, the merchants. I'm making more money than I ever dreamed of, besides my salary."

"Some aren't happy," she suggested.

He waved that aside. "They can blame themselves, and the town fathers like Frank Dane."

"And who do you blame?"

He stared, answered explosively, "Them!"

"Then ride along with Jerry, if that's the way it is."

He walked slowly to the chair and sat down. "I want to stay," he said at last. "What else is there?"

She looked at her hands as she spoke. "We can always go somewhere else, Roy."

"Where can I do better than right here?"

"That didn't use to be so important."

"It is now!" he snapped.

"Then don't buck Jerry Hecker." There was an edge in her voice. "That's a sure way to lose your money, and your life. Take his orders and you'll get everything you want, including Alice Dane."

He looked up. "You know what little Alice Dane really means to me."

"Do I?" Her eyes were pleading. "You've got a good income and a steady job. You have me, like you've always had." Her voice grew bitter. "Why wouldn't I make as good a wife as Alice Dane?"

He was at her side in an instant. She tried to jerk her hands free of his, but he held them tightly. "Hallie! Hallie! I've told you how it is. If I have position and respect in this town, I won't need Jerry Hecker. Frank Dane is as wealthy as the banker, and it will all go to her. Why shouldn't I get a chance at it? Some man will."

"Position! Power! Money!" she exclaimed. "My God, how you've changed!"

He spoke quietly, seriously. "You can blame this town, then. It taught me I was a fool to have all those fine big notions about a law badge. So I figure money is just as important to me. I intend to get it."

"It's wrong, Roy!"

"Is it? Look at yourself—making dresses for women who won't talk to you on the street. Why? Because you work for them!"

"No! It's because you won't—" She broke off, eyes misting.

"How can I? Sheriff and all that, and—"

"I live at the edge of town and people whisper about me," she bitterly finished for him.

They were silent, Cantro still holding her hands. "Hallie, we'll always be together. Don't worry about Alice Dane. You're the one I love and you know it."

He tried to kiss her. She ran from the chair and was across the room in a flurry of skirts. She turned, face flushed. "You'd better go, Roy."

"But—"

"I'm tired. I . . . Just go!"

He stood a moment and then picked his hat up from the floor. He went to the door, looked expectantly back at her, but Hallie remained silent and unmoving. He rolled the hat brim around in his hands.

"I've told you about this before. You know that. I told you then like I'm telling you now that I love—"

"Please go!" she cut in, her voice tight and vibrating.

He went out. The door closed softly behind him. Suddenly Hallie's face convulsed in utter hatred. She heard the steady, fading beat of Cantro's horse. Then complete silence.

Her throat moved spasmodically. The tears brimmed over and she buried her face in her hands. She turned blindly and stumbled into the dark bedroom.

Chapter X

A few mornings later, Breck walked toward the barn, whistling silently as he considered plans for building up the Circle M. It would be a long and hard process but it could be done, if . . . The passing thought of Hecker made him frown.

He heard a distant hail from the road. A rider jogged into the ranch yard and Breck recognized Matt Unger with a surge of excitement. Matt would only come if something had developed. He waited for Matt at the big hitchrack. Matt eased out of the saddle and looked about sharply. "Had any more sudden visitors?"

"They're leaving me alone."

"Biding their time."

Matt accompanied Breck into the house. He looked about, sighed and accepted a whiskey. "Last I was here, Jim was counting up his losses." He placed the glass on the desk. "Still willing to run for sheriff and risk a bullet?"

Breck nodded. "More than ever. Point is, are your friends willing to back me?"

Matt stood up. "Come over to my place—say, tomorrow night. You'll find out who your friends are in these parts. They want to see and talk to you."

"Look for me, Matt."

"Right after nightfall," Matt suggested.

Breck went with him to the hitchrack. Matt swung into the saddle easily and rode off at an ambling pace. Breck watched him go, pleased by the news and yet sensing that all was not yet fully settled.

The next day, Breck rode the range toward San Alma, eyes alert for any sign of the outlaws. He rode to his ranch line and then followed it toward the San Alma road. Not long after, he suddenly drew rein. Some distance ahead, a saddled horse browsed under a tree. Breck could not see its owner and his hand dropped to his gun as he cast about for a possible ambush.

He moved in slowly. The grazing horse suddenly looked up, ears pricking forward, and whinnied. Breck reined in, hand darting to his gun, as a figure appeared from around the tree. He looked in surprise at Hallie Yates.

Her magnificent eyes widened as she saw the gun leveled at her. Breck hastily dropped it into the holster and swung out of the saddle. Hallie recovered her composure and looked at him with a little half smile.

"Am I that dangerous, Mr. Malone?"

"I hope not, ma'am. I didn't see you and I thought—"

"I was one of Jerry Hecker's friends?" she finished. "I hardly think that's flattering. Do you?"

He smiled. "I reckon it's not, after a good look at you."

"Why, thank you! I guess I shouldn't be on Circle M range."

"No harm."

There was a faint redness about her eyes, as though she might have cried recently. She moved to her horse and picked up the reins, hesitated, and then turned to Breck. "Do you know who I am?"

"Sure. Hallie Yates."

"I don't mean that. Do you know *about* me?"

"You make dresses for people around San Alma."

She seemed to force out the question, "Have you heard talk about me?"

Breck felt uncomfortable. "Why, as to that . . ."

"I want the truth, Mr. Malone."

He saw the mounting red in her cheeks. "You can hear talk about everyone, but you can't stop it. So you don't listen."

"But it gets around," she said bitterly.

"So does a snake. I always figure I'm the best judge of someone. I take a person for what he seems to be. Sometimes I make mistakes, but that's my fault."

She looked searchingly at him. "I had forgotten such honesty existed."

She looked at him so long and searchingly that he shifted uncomfortably. Then she moved about the horse and was in the saddle before he could help her. She smiled down at him. "Mr. Malone, I would like very much to tell you something. I think you are exactly the right man for Alice Dane, and she's your kind of woman. I think you should do something about it, Mr. Malone."

She touched spurs and the horse galloped off, heading toward the San Alma road. Breck slowly walked back to his horse. He frowned, wondering why she wanted him to win Alice when she must know this would bring direct conflict with Cantro. Why should she run the chance of putting him in danger if she was, secretly, his girl?

Slowly, Breck began to understand. He could imagine how she'd felt when the sheriff started courting Alice. That would

75

explain the red about her eyes and her wish for him and Alice.

Hallie faced a devil's choice: Cantro married to Alice or Cantro maybe dead and so, in a sense, hers forever. Perhaps she hoped that Cantro would come out of the inevitable gun clash unscathed, or wounded at the most. This might make him give up his plans.

Breck rode slowly toward the ranch house, thinking of Alice. She *was* his kind of woman. He determined to see Frank Dane and try to win him over. He thought of Cantro and knew there was nothing he could do. They would meet head-on. It was certain as the sun.

That night, an hour after full dark, Breck rode into the Unger ranch yard. Once again he was halted.

"They're waiting for you," the guard said. He turned to a companion. "Show him the way."

Puzzled, Breck sank back in the saddle until the guard, mounted now, drifted up and ordered him to follow. They were soon out on Unger's range, heading almost due north.

The range gave way to the Thunders that loomed against the sky, blackening out the stars. The going grew rougher. The guide never faltered, making surprising turns, threading canyons, crossing small meadows and plunging into canyons again.

They emerged into one of these meadows and the guide stopped. He whistled a few bars of a cowboy lament and immediately the tune was picked up by someone close ahead in the darkness. A man appeared, afoot, a rifle cradled in his arm. The guide said, "I brought him. You taking him in?"

"That's right."

The guide turned his horse and, without a word, disappeared into the night. The other man spoke softly, "Follow me."

Breck kept his horse's nose close to the man's shadow. The canyon closed about them and then fell away. A horse whinnied and Breck realized there must be twenty or more of them picketed in the dark shadows of the canyon's wall.

"Leave your horse here," the guide ordered.

Breck swung out of the saddle and followed the guide. They entered another canyon. It made a turn and Breck saw a fire, its light filling every cranny of a pocket. About twenty men were revealed, shielded by the high canyon walls.

Doc Vance and Matt Unger stepped from the crowd to meet him, Unger grasping his hand. "We've been waiting for you, Breck. Some of the men were getting nervous."

Breck looked around the pocket. "I never expected anything like this."

"Do you think a crowd wouldn't be noticed at Matt's house?" Doc Vance demanded. "Jerry Hecker's not one to sleep, and we know it. Come on, meet the bunch."

Each man briefly shook Breck's hand and he felt their searching, weighing looks as a word was spoken and he moved on to the next.

At last, Unger stepped to the fire and cleared his throat. "Breck, these gents hope you're the one to do something for San Alma. They've risked a lot just to come here. Point is, they've heard about you, but that ain't enough. If they're going to risk an all-out fight against Hecker, they want to make damn sure about the cut of your pants."

"What can I tell them?"

"Just answer their questions." Unger grinned. "And they got a heap of them."

"I'm ready."

The men fired questions at him like bullets and Breck answered, fully and honestly. By the time the long session was over, they had some idea of his background, his adventures along the border, his reasons for coming back. More important, they knew why he fought Hecker and they were impressed. They had some idea of his courage. They looked at one another questioningly and then Lashlee spoke up.

"Malone, we'd like to talk this over, among ourselves. Any objection?"

Without a word, Breck walked into the darkness of the canyon. Beyond the turn was a small area between the canyon walls. He could hear nothing, but he knew the debate swung back and forth. Its result would definitely shape the immediate future, not only for him, but for all San Alma.

Decision one way meant concerted action to free San Alma of the shadow of the outlaws. Decision another way meant that Breck would face a lone and desperate fight against Hecker. One way or the other, the showdown would soon come.

Breck whipped around when Lashlee spoke from the turn in the canyon. He strode back to the fire and faced the group, an impassive face hiding his tension. Matt acted as their spokesman.

"Breck, we'll back you. You stay close to Circle M like you have been. Each of these gents will start spreading word to people he can trust in such a way that nothing will get back to Hecker."

"How about filing?" Breck asked.

"There'll be enough signatures so the county clerk will have to accept the filing. We'll have every decent citizen backing you."

Unger turned to the group. "Everything depends on surprise. We come out in the open on filing day. You can bet if Hecker finds out before we're organized, he'll smash us before we have a chance."

John Dean spoke quietly. "In union is strength, remember? And in secrecy, success. It's our only chance."

The men promised to round up support in their various areas and to make certain no word leaked. The fire was doused and the group walked down the canyon to their horses, then moved out in one's and two's. Soon only Matt Unger and Doc Vance remained with Breck. The three mounted and moved slowly along the dark and winding way.

They spoke of the coming deadline for filing. Unger thought Breck should have more hands at the Circle M as defense against Hecker.

Breck dissented. "Hecker would know something's wrong. I can barely keep my two boys busy as it is. Trouble will come right in town. One of his gundogs will pick a fight, or there'll be a bushwhack along a road or on my range. You can't get enough men to guard against things like that."

Unger realized Breck was right. Nearing his ranch, he rode off in the darkness while Breck and Doc Vance continued on toward Circle M. They came to the main road to San Alma and Doc Vance reined in. "I leave you here."

"Come to the house? A drink?"

"Nope, too late. An old man likes to turn in early." He eased back in the saddle. "I knew they'd back you, Breck, once they saw what you're like. But now that you know you're going after Cantro's job, what do you intend to do about Alice Dane?"

Breck straightened in surprise. "Alice! What do you know about me and her?"

"Why, boy, I know how much in love she was before you rode off yonderly. You've been to her house twice since you've been back. Though neither you nor Cantro said as much, I know jealousy was back of your fight and arrest. It was pretty plain."

"I guess it was," Breck admitted, embarrassed.

"Breck, you get that girl right away. She's been waiting all these years for you to pop the question."

"You're forgetting her father. He doesn't like me."

"Pay no attention to him. Marrying Alice off might pull him out of a bind."

"What do you mean?"

"Frank Dane isn't in on this election deal. Roy Cantro is welcome at his house—and Cantro always means Jerry Hecker somewhere in the background."

"Are you saying—"

"No proof, mind you, but Dane is the only merchant who's not complaining about the renegades. Some say he deals with them."

"I'd never figure Frank to be crooked!"

"Did you figure Cantro to be what he is?"

"No."

"Something sure changed him. And something changed Frank Dane. Something to think about, Breck. Good night. Stick close to Circle M and you'll hear from us."

He faded into the darkness and Breck continued slowly on to Circle M. He was surprised and concerned about this rumor, scoffed at it and then realized how it explained Frank's anger when he found his daughter turning from Cantro.

The ranch buildings appeared ahead, black shadows against a dark sky. The boys had long since turned in, but there would be one of them on guard. Breck sang out his name as he rode toward the house and then saw the faint gleam of light against a drawn blind. That would be Tip.

Breck off-saddled and walked toward the house, his thoughts again on Frank Dane. If the rumors about him were true, it would make a mean situation. Alice was loyal to her father and might not go against his wishes.

Breck stepped up on the porch, opened the door, took a step inside and pulled up short. Jerry Hecker sat in a big chair, facing him. He held a whiskey glass in his hand.

"Evening, Malone. I've been a long time waiting. But I made myself at home."

Chapter XI

THE BLACK MUZZLE of the Colt, held steadily in Jerry's right hand, was lined on Breck. He reached slowly behind him and closed the door, shooting a glance across the room to the dimly lit hallway.

Jerry's smile widened. "There's just the two of us. Lift your Colt, slow and easy. Drop it on the floor."

Breck stood a second and saw the faint hardening of Jerry's jaw. He carefully removed the gun from the holster and let it fall to the rug.

"Now kick it to me."

With a flick of his foot, Breck sent the gun spinning across the floor to Jerry's feet. The outlaw placed it on the table, close to his hand, then holstered his own gun.

"Sit down, Breck, and have a drink. After all, this is your place."

"So it is," Breck said dryly, "and I didn't expect company."

"I decided to drop in. Didn't think you'd be gone."

Breck walked to the stand against the wall and poured a drink from the bottle, his movements covering the quick churn of his thoughts. He knew that Jerry might be aware of the meeting in the canyon or of Breck's decision to openly challenge Cantro in the election.

He turned. "Where's your watchdog?"

"Chulo? He's keeping your boys company in the bunkhouse."

Breck sat down, certain that there must be more of the renegades about, probably just outside. He wondered how many of their guns had been trained on him as he rode in the yard.

But the real threat sat at ease in the chair before him. Breck adopted Jerry's casual tone, hiding his tension and alarm. "Something on your mind, Hecker? This ain't a friendly call."

"Now what would there be on my mind?" Jerry asked. "You're sure filled with suspicion."

"I can think of Red Hollings—or the two boys who got themselves shot."

Jerry dropped back in the chair, but his right hand was

never far from Breck's gun on the table. "Yes, you owe me a debt there. But I don't think this is the time to bring it up."

"Then it's about the ranch."

"Why, there's a lot of things for us to talk about. Make yourself comfortable, Malone. We might be here a long while."

Jerry smoothed his thin mustache and contentedly studied the amber color of his whiskey. But Breck sensed coiled danger. He eased back in his chair, deciding to let Jerry set the pace.

Jerry emptied his glass and placed it beside the gun.

"Malone, you've given me a lot of trouble. Still, there's something about you I like."

"But not enough to forget the trouble," Breck added.

Jerry chuckled. "Not for good, anyhow. You interest me for several reasons. You're a fast man with a gun, as Red Hollings can prove. You shoot pretty straight in a hurry and I lost two men because of it. You take care of yourself. Roy Cantro found that out."

Breck shrugged. "You can say the same about a lot of men, good or bad."

"Maybe—but there's something more. You have a knack of making people like you. I've seen it."

"Now where's this heading?"

"I don't know. That's why I'm here, Malone. I keep thinking what a damn shame it is we keep bucking one another. Fast gun and accurate, good with your fists—something I always look for in a man. Add that to the way you make friends, it's pretty unbeatable. I'm like that, too, but I guess you've seen that yourself."

Breck grinned. Jerry's complete assurance of his own superiority was part of his ability to handle his wolf pack. He had no need to notch guns or act dangerously to prove himself. He thoroughly knew his own capabilities and character, and was quite satisfied. But it also marked him as potentially far more dangerous than his gunslingers.

Breck rose slowly and spoke over his shoulder as he refilled his glass. "In one way, I can say it's been a pleasure to meet you. I've never seen a man who looked less like his reputation. You look more like a hardware drummer than an outlaw."

Jerry smiled his appreciation. "I like good clothes, good manners—now that I can afford 'em."

"More brains than the usual run," Breck said, considering him. "I think you could've been a success in anything. How come you went outside the law?"

Jerry sucked in his cheeks, not at all offended.

"What makes a man become anything, Malone? Things happen, people shape him maybe. I was always one who liked to break the rules, or make his own. It amounts to the same thing. Something in the way you think, I reckon, or in your blood."

"Like a disease?"

The green eyes flicked at Breck like a serpent's tongue and then Jerry laughed. "Who's sicker than a man eating his heart out for things he can have for the taking? But, hell! I want to talk about you, not me."

Breck waited, eyes level. Jerry moved irritably and finally leaned forward. "Malone, I figured I'd have your answer about this place before now."

"Say, right after the raid, Hecker? Force is a poor way to persuade a man."

"It works with some. Not with you. I should've figured that. Now I know you better and so I'm going to talk like one reasonable man to another. I take it you weigh one thing against another before you make a decision?"

Breck nodded, concealing his thoughts. Jerry continued after a moment. "Take San Alma, for instance, and the way things are here. You know by now what your chances are of staying on Circle M."

"Back to threats again," Breck said dryly.

"No, something different. I'm not fool enough to figure there's just one way to get what I want. So I've been thinking about you. Maybe there's some way both of us can get along and each come out okay."

"Now what do *I* want?" Breck asked with a faint sarcasm.

"To stay here on Circle M. Jim Malone willed it to you and you feel you ought to hold on. But there's still more to it. For ten years you've been fiddlefooting and you want to settle down. Am I right?"

"Say you are—then what?"

"You'd like to make something of Circle M. Build it up. It'd make you independent and you'd be a pretty big man in San Alma."

"But you wanted to buy me out, or drive me out."

"Sure. And I can still go either way. But I'm not one to stick to a plan if there's a better one. I see a way you and I can get along, and it'll make you the biggest rancher in San Alma. Are you interested?"

Breck stretched out his long legs. He knew he had no chance, disarmed, to get to Hecker. Each time he had moved, he'd noticed the outlaw's hand tense, ready to grab the gun. Recognizing this, Breck began to find a perverse enjoyment in sparring with Hecker, seeking to draw him out. Breck could not agree with the renegade and yet he knew that an open refusal could easily mean a bullet.

He pursed his lips and spoke slowly. "'Be the biggest rancher,'" he repeated. "Let's see what that would mean. First, a lot more beef than I've got now."

"That's right."

"Rustled, maybe. Stuff your boys would run in. Slap my brand on them. There'd probably be horses, too, but I wouldn't get much use of them. You'd want 'em for fast remounts and always handy in case of trouble. I'd sell the cattle and you'd get a cut. I'd probably get a little extra for taking care of the horses. Maybe I'd even be cut in on some of the other stuff. Is that what you have in mind?"

Jerry laughed appreciatively. "Close, Malone. You're no fool. But there's more'n that. I figure you'd buy and sell cattle over the country."

"That takes ready cash."

"Why, that's no problem. I can put all you need in your pocket."

Breck leaned forward, elbows on his knees, hands hanging limp. His voice sounded sharp, caustic. "No one's that generous, Hecker. You've figured some way of getting it back."

"Sure, you sell the cattle, you pay off. But you could forget the whole thing if, on your travels, you happened to find a likely bank or heard about a bullion shipment or a mine payroll. You look so damned honest and people like you. They'd talk. There's a dozen ways we could get along, Malone."

Breck remained unmoving, studying him. "You sure make it sound good."

"I'm trying to." Jerry seemed to have forgotten the gun, but Breck wasn't fooled by that. "There's no end to what we could do, working together."

"I can see one end—dying by rope or bullet."

"We're too smart for that, and you're too good with a gun to be caught." Jerry added quickly, "Not that you'll take a hand with the bunch. We'll take the risks and you get your share."

Breck stared at him a long moment and straightened. Instantly, Jerry's fingers tensed and taloned, not yet taking agreement and friendship for granted. Breck smiled bleakly and again walked to the stand. This time he needed the cleansing burn of the whiskey to control his anger.

He looked back at Jerry. The smooth, round face was without mark of dissipation or evil. The smile was still the

83

friendly, warm thing that Breck had first noticed about him. Only in the quick, sharp glitter of the eyes did the real character of the man show, and then fleetingly.

Breck turned around, leaned against the stand. "Ever read the Bible, Hecker?"

The outlaw looked surprised and then gave a twisted smile. "Malone! You're not going to preach a sermon?"

"No. But you remind me of the Devil. He was always offering everything in sight and making it sound easy."

Jerry's eyes danced. "Now there's a gent I admire, from what I've heard of him. So what are you going to do about *my* offer?"

"Funny thing about the Devil. He kept running up against honest men and he couldn't slap his brand on 'em."

"Damn fools, you mean!"

"I don't know about them, but I guess you could say that about me. Honesty's a funny thing, Hecker. You can't see it or touch it, but it's always getting in the way, time and again. It's one of my habits now and I can't break it. More'n that, I don't want to."

Jerry's eyes narrowed slightly. "I never figured you for a fool."

Breck returned to his chair. "What makes a fool? You're not, for certain, but there's something you've completely missed."

"What?"

"Something inside that makes a man feel he can look any other man straight in the face, that his word's good, that he doesn't have to lie or run from anyone. Self-respect —I guess that's the best word for it."

"Malone, most men are honest because they haven't the guts or imagination to be anything else. But just show 'em a way to make a lot of money and see how fast they go after it."

"You have a damn low opinion of people."

"Why not? They're double-talking fools for the most part."

Breck's expression showed his disbelief. It annoyed Jerry. "I can name a dozen in San Alma who talk big and fine in public but make deals with me on the quiet. You'd be surprised."

"A dozen," Breck said softly, then asked sharply. "Out of how many?"

Jerry disregarded the question. "If a man bothers to think, he soon sees there's not much difference in the ways a man makes money or gets ahead. Rich or poor, sooner or later you're planted six feet under. So there's just one important thing—get what you can while you can."

"There you ride one trail and I ride another."

"And where are we? I'm riding high and fine and can do what I please. I get what I want and do what I want. What have you got?"

"Circle M."

"Until I decide to take over. What else?"

"That other thing that I spoke about and you don't understand. I can live with myself and I'm not afraid to face any man."

Jerry looked at him a long moment. Then he stood up and pitched Breck's gun far across the room onto the horsehide sofa, further away than ever. He walked to the stand and poured himself a drink, never taking his eyes from Breck.

"We keep riding around one another and don't meet. You're the first man I've ever spent so much time on, but you're worth a lot more working *with* me than dead. I figure you're a man who'll come around to my way of thinking, being smart as you are."

"And inviting a bullet if I don't?"

Jerry downed his drink. "We haven't got that far yet. But anyway you take it, one of three things is bound to happen. You can fight me and that'll end in Boothill—for you. It'd be a sad waste of a good man and I don't like it."

"Amen!"

"You can sell Circle M and move out. I'd settle for that, but there's a better way. Keep the ranch and work with me. I've given you some ideas as to how it would work."

"I've said how it wouldn't."

Hecker moved to the door. "Malone, I won't take that as final. You haven't turned the idea around and about like you should. A lot to win there against a lot to lose. Take a look at Circle M and then at San Alma's Boothill. It's that simple."

Breck threw a swift, longing glance toward his gun, then back to the outlaw. "You keep trying to make deals."

"Because you interest me. I can use you. I can wait for your decision. I'll be in San Alma a long, long while. But time can run out for you, Malone."

He was quick to see the hardening of Breck's jaw, the flash in the gray eyes. Jerry set his hat at a jaunty angle and his even teeth flashed in a wide smile.

"Man, I'm offering, not threatening! And I can add something else that might mean a lot more than all the rest. There's a girl in town. I could make things mighty easy for you."

Breck broke into a laugh. "Hecker, that's one promise you

can't deliver. Alice Dane will make up her own mind and there's nothing you can do."

Now Jerry smiled. "You're forgetting Roy Cantro. He could go right out of the picture, if I say so."

"Cantro might have different ideas."

"Oh, he does! But he follows my orders or . . . Well, I've had my say. Think it over, but don't let my patience wear thin."

Breck nodded, his expression telling nothing. Jerry slid his Colt from the holster and once more lined it on him. "We'll go to the bunkhouse now. Might be Chulo has upset your boys. It'd be a shame if they tried to spoil a friendly evening."

Breck looked at the gun. "You've persuaded me."

Jerry stepped away from the door. Breck walked out onto the porch, Jerry just behind him, the gun pointed at the small of his back. As they crossed the porch, Jerry gave a peculiar whistle.

Instantly a shadow moved and a man materialized at the far corner of the house. Another came out of the darkness near the corral. The four of them, Breck leading the way, walked to the bunkhouse. At a word from Jerry, one of the men walked toward the barn, where hidden, saddled horses waited.

Breck opened the bunkhouse door, blinked against the light. Chulo Wyeth sat at a table, working on a solitaire layout, his Colt at hand, the metal coldly reflecting the lamplight. The big gunman's muddy eyes rested on Breck a moment and then moved to Jerry just behind him. Breck saw Tip and his riders sitting on the bunks, hands tied behind their backs. Tip had a bruise on his jaw and his lips were tightly closed, though his eyes blazed.

"No trouble?" Jerry asked.

Chulo stood up. "The old one tried to sass, but I taught him better. Made him tie up the rest and then I took care of him. How about you?"

"Friendly, Chulo, very friendly. We'll be riding now."

"How about them?" Chulo's gesture included Breck and the crew.

"How about it, Malone?" Jerry asked.

"You've got the guns."

"Remember it."

Through the open door, Breck heard horses being led up. Jerry signalled Chulo outside. When the big gunman walked out, Jerry backed to the door. He made a slight movement with the gun and smiled.

"Be smart, Malone. Stand hitched for a while."

He closed the door then. Breck swung half around, then checked his angry step. He had no gun, and no weapon was in sight. Bullets would blast him down in a second if he rushed outside.

He stood with fists clenched as he heard the sudden drumming lift of hoof beats. They faded and were gone. Breck turned to the bunks and released the men.

Tip's blazing eyes met his and the foreman spoke through set teeth. "When a showdown comes, I get Chulo Wyeth. I don't care who handles the others, but I want him."

Breck tugged at the ropes around Tip's wrists. "You won't have to wait long, Tip. Not long at all."

Chapter XII

CHULO WYETH had thrown the men's guns far out into the ranch yard and it took a long time to find them. Even so, Tip wanted to go after the outlaws, anger blinding him to the fact that they had little chance of picking up the trail in the dark. With some difficulty, Breck persuaded him, Lew and Chuck to forget the outlaws until morning. He took them to the house and poured drinks around, saw reason gradually gain ascendancy over fury.

He told them the main reason for Jerry's visit, the alternatives of working with the outlaw or facing violent death. They listened, Tip with mounting anger but with no doubt as to Breck's decision, the other two with faint uncertainty.

"Hecker had a gun on me," Breck finished. "He had only to pull the trigger if he knew for certain I'd fight him."

"Will you?" Lew asked.

Tip whipped around, eyes blazing. "Is that all you know about the Malones?"

"I'm not selling the ranch nor working with him," Breck said. "I'm not riding off and letting him take over. But I sure don't intend to land in Boothill."

Lew's face cleared. Chuck grinned and nodded. "That's all we wanted to know, Breck. High time someone stood up to that bunch. Count us in."

Breck thanked them, poured another drink. The crew returned to the bunkhouse and Breck walked to the sofa and picked up his gun. He looked at it a moment, balanced it, and then, grimly, slid it into the holster.

The next morning, Breck rode to Matt Unger's ranch, feeling that it was important that the rancher should know what had happened. Matt was surprised to see him, sensing real trouble behind the visit. He and Breck stood at the corral, to all appearances talking cattle prices or the weather. Matt listened to the story, frowning toward the high peaks of the Thunders.

"He sure laid the cards down and put his chips on 'em," he said when Breck finished. "Good thing you didn't let on last night you'd have no truck with him."

"You don't talk back to a gun muzzle."

"That's sure! When are you supposed to let him know?"

"He didn't say, but he won't wait long."

Matt swore. "We've got to have more time! Can't have a showdown now. We're just getting started and Hecker would rip us apart before we could protect one another."

"That's what I figure. The longer I can stall, the better organized and stronger we get."

"Can you, though?"

"I think so. You come down to it, Hecker sees a lot more advantage in me alive than dead—if there's a chance I'll throw in."

"Mmmm . . . and filing day's not far off."

"I'll try to hold him off until then."

Matt warned, "Then don't go to town too often. Stay out of his way and he won't have a chance to call your hand."

"If I stay away too long, he'll know I'm putting him off. I'd better show up in San Alma for supplies and an occasional Saturday night or he'll be riding out to the ranch again."

"But what'll you say to him?"

"I don't know. I'll keep him dangling, one way or another. Better get word around, Matt. Maybe we can get organized faster than we think."

"I'll do that."

Breck rode home and remained close to the ranch. The following Saturday, he sent the boys into town. They were back by nightfall, cutting short their fun to guard against trouble at the ranch.

The next week went slowly. No one sent word to Breck, nor did he see any sign of the outlaws. But time grew short and he braced himself for a meeting with Hecker. He felt helpless, for there was nothing he could do except let the days go by. It was a momentary stalemate.

He could do nothing about Hecker except wait for developments, but he felt that he should not delay so far as Alice was concerned. He had been away from San Alma too long and, despite Matt's advice, he felt he should see the girl. It was more—an almost overwhelming longing. He thought of her many times and, when Saturday came again, he was as eager as any of the crew to saddle up and ride in.

As they approached the edge of town, Tip gave him a sidelong glance. "Do we shed our Colts again?"

"Not this time."

"Now that's a change of tune!"

Breck grinned. "Maybe Hecker will want an answer, if he's in town. If he forces it, I want a gun where I can get it."

"Hope he does, and Chulo with him!"

89

"Don't look for trouble, Tip. Lew . . . Chuck . . . that goes for you, too."

"Now what's the use of wearing a gun and—"

Breck cut in on Lew's complaint. "We're avoiding a fight now. But it won't be long before we can call taws. I'll tell you when. But for now, walk around trouble."

Lew shrugged, but accepted the order. Breck rode with them to the courthouse and, with a final warning, left them there and rode slowly to the side street where the Dane home stood. He swung out of the saddle and ground-tied the horse. He started up the walk, then stopped short when the door opened and Alice stood framed.

She wore a plain, gray gingham dress, but it looked beautiful to Breck, accenting her graceful height, seeming to deepen the violet in her eyes, making the color in her cheeks more lovely. She smiled with a touch of fright. Then her chin lifted and she came to the edge of the porch as he bounded up the steps.

She read his intent to kiss her in his eyes and she spoke swiftly. "Come in, Breck."

She turned and walked inside, Breck just behind her. Within the hallway, safe from curious eyes along the street, she whirled about and came to his arms, lifting her lips.

After a moment, she stepped back, breathless, and again alarmed. "You shouldn't have come. Father is still furious."

"Is he here?"

"At the store. He's awfully mad at you—and me."

"I'd like to talk to him."

"It's a bad time. He'd order you out this minute if he were here."

Breck put his hands on her shoulders. "What can we do about it?"

"I don't know. Wait until I can bring him around. I'm trying, every chance I get."

Breck spoke softly. "I think this is something for you and me to decide. I never had the chance the other time to ask you to marry me. Will you?"

Her eyes lighted with a wonderful glow and her lips parted. Then a shadow came over her and she looked uncertain. "I . . . Breck, I don't know."

"You don't want to?"

"Oh, but I do!"

"Then it's Frank—or Roy Cantro."

"You know it's not Roy! It's Father. We've been so close. It just doesn't seem fair to do anything now while he's so upset. He'd never forgive me."

Breck could not conceal his disappointment and she smiled

90

softly and gave his arm a reassuring squeeze. He bit at his lip. "What has Frank against me?"

She sat down on the sofa, Breck beside her. She sighed. "I wish I knew. I've never seen him so angry as he was the other night. We had an awful quarrel, the first we've ever had. Now he won't even let me mention your name."

"How long can this go on?"

"I don't know. I can't hurt him."

"I understand. Main thing is that—"

"I love you," she cut in. "I can hardly remember when I haven't."

"That's all I need to know."

He kissed her and stood up. She looked at him in alarm, sensing that he had come to some decision. He smiled at her. "I think we can work this out some way."

"Breck, you're not angry with me?"

In answer, he kissed her and turned to the door. He hurried to his horse and swung into the saddle. She stood at the edge of the porch, worriedly watching him. He made a reassuring gesture and rode down the street. As he turned the corner, he looked back, saw her still on the porch, looking after him.

He cut around the courthouse and approached the business district. He saw, with a passing sense of relief, that there were few horses tied to the hitchrack before the Cattleman. Either the wild bunch was again on one of its mysterious trips or it was too early in the day for them to make their appearance. He looked toward Cantro's office, almost turned in, then changed his mind and rode on to the Dane store and dismounted.

There were few customers in the store—a lull in the usual rush of Saturday business. Frank Dane was not behind the counter and Breck walked down the aisle to the small office. Dane looked up from the desk as Breck stood in the doorway. The man's eyes widened for a second and then his lips pressed angrily as he frowned.

He spoke coldly. "Morning, Malone."

"I'd like to talk to you, Frank."

The merchant swung around to the desk and the ledger in which he had been making entries. "This is a bad time, Malone."

"It's a good time." Breck stepped inside and closed the door. Dane swung around, angry. "Make it short, then."

"Frank, ten years ago you liked me fine and I remember how you used to kid me about Alice, like you were pleased she took a fancy to me. I didn't know then how I felt about

91

her, but I do now. I can't figure why you order me out of the house and tell me not to see her."

Dane's fingers beat an angry tattoo on the desk. "That's my business, and she's my daughter. But I will say that time and people change. Is that all, Malone?"

He glared at Breck, expecting him to leave. Breck remained standing by the door, unmoving. Dane's eyes slid away, came back again, an edge of uncertainty in the challenging stare.

"We're not wasting time, Frank. This is damn important to both of us. As to change, that hasn't happened to Alice. We're in love. I want to marry her and I'd like your consent."

Dane sprang to his feet, fists clenched. "I won't have it! I won't listen to it! She'll do as I say, do you hear!"

His face grew red and suffused. He took a step toward Breck, eyes glaring, lips working. Breck stood impassive and Dane checked himself. Breck listened to the man's invective, but once again he felt that Frank's anger hid something else. It triggered too quickly, became too great, and so it held a slightly false note. Breck would have been far more inclined to believe the old man had Dane quietly but firmly stated his opposition.

By now, Frank fairly trembled. He pointed to the door. "Malone, I don't want you here any more than I do at home. Get out!"

"Frank, I wish this could be some other way."

"It'll never be!"

"You're wrong. I've come to you open and square to tell you how Alice and I feel. You won't listen and you won't say why."

"Of course I won't—"

"Then listen to this, Frank. I'm going to marry Alice, with or without your consent." Breck's gray eyes narrowed and his voice grew calm. "Something's changed you, Frank. It's not good and I wonder what it is. Something's making you afraid."

Dane's face went slack. His hand moved blindly behind him, touched the desk, and gripped its edge. He searched Breck's face with a strange expression compounded of guilt, pleading and withdrawal. His lips worked and, for a second, Breck knew he was on the edge of revelation. Then fear returned, shaking him until he replaced it once more with the disguise of anger. He moistened his lips.

"Get out, Malone! I . . . I'll call the sheriff!"

"All right, Frank. You've got that right. But this won't end it."

Breck opened the door and walked out, leaving Dane by the desk, his body straight and tense. Breck strode out into the street. He looked back into the shadowy store, unmindful of the curious glances of passers-by. He felt less anger than puzzled disappointment. He had hoped there might be a chance to reason with Frank, even though Alice had told him her father was still angry. Now he realized Frank was adamant and could easily prevent the marriage for a while. Not forever, Breck knew, but at least until Alice finally saw she could not bring her father around.

But beyond this disappointment lay the puzzling lack of reason for the old man's attitude. Breck recalled Doc Vance's hints about Frank. The merchant's anger had validity only if the rumors were true.

Apparently Frank wanted Cantro as a future son-in-law, or was being forced to accept him as such. Breck felt certain that word of the quarrel would eventually reach the sheriff, as would the news that he had called on Alice again. Gossip has a way of travelling fast and twisting facts unless it is prevented.

Breck, jaw set, walked directly to the sheriff's office, pushed open the door and walked in. The room was empty and Breck was about to leave when Cantro appeared from the cell corridor. He stopped short in surprise, caught himself and came on to the desk. He glanced beyond Breck out the open door, as though expecting trouble.

His black eyes cut back to Breck. "Malone?"

Breck closed the door and a small frown appeared on Cantro's forehead. Breck said, levelly, "I don't think you'll like what I have to say."

"It's become a habit. What kind of trouble have you cooked up now?"

"I just left Frank Dane. We were talking about Alice."

Cantro grinned, an unpleasant move of the lips. "I can figure how much good that did you!"

"We had words. You'll hear about 'em. I reckon you'll also be told I was with Alice a time this morning."

Cantro's fingers slowly folded into a fist, but there was no other reaction. He waited.

"I wanted to tell you myself, Cantro, so this time you'll know I'm not going behind your back. I talked to her and then I saw Frank. He wouldn't listen to what I had to say."

Again Cantro smiled and his voice was acid. "So you wasted your time."

"Not quite. I figure you ought to know what I told him. It's something between us, Cantro, that neither you nor Frank can change. I'm going to marry her. Count on it."

93

Silence built up in the room. Cantro remained unmoving, his black eyes searching Breck, seeming to stab and shift as they grew harder. Then a glitter appeared far back in them.

Breck broke the silence. "Now we know where we stand."

He turned to leave, but the sudden, blazing fury in Cantro's pale face was a warning. The sheriff spoke with deadly intensity.

"I'm going to kill you."

Chapter XIII

THEY STOOD FACE TO FACE across the small area of the office. Breck's hand hung just below his holster, fingers slightly spread, ready for the swift, blurring motion that would snap the Colt out of leather.

He watched Cantro's eyes, knowing the first faint signal would lie there. Cantro's right arm was slightly akimbo, hand hovering over the plain walnut grip of his gun. His lips were strangely bloodless and immobile and his fury had been swept away by the cold, deadly precision of the gun fighter. Breck knew that at any second he would catch that faint flick of eye and muscle that signalled blasting gunfire and death for one of them.

Hurried steps broke the tension and the door banged back as Frank Dane burst into the room. He plowed to a halt, face slack with surprise, filled with fear when he saw the way the two men faced one another.

Breck's eyes never left Cantro. The sheriff jerked, as though Dane's entrance had touched some spring or hidden button. His face remained set and gaunt for a second and then his right hand slowly dropped to his side.

His voice still held a vibrant, tight quality as he spoke. "Something wrong, Frank?"

Dane's head jerked to him and then back to Breck, fright showing openly now. He swallowed and found his voice.

"Just . . . wanted to see you."

Cantro blazed at Breck. "Twice you've been lucky, Malone. But later—you can depend on it—later. . . ."

"There are other ways, Cantro. But it's however you want it."

He turned to the door. Dane looked confused and, now that his fright and surprise had ebbed, embarrassed. Breck smiled tightly.

"I've just told him, Frank."

He walked out before Dane or Cantro could reply. He did not look back as he crossed the street to the Thunder. That had been close, and now he felt the backlash of tension. He had only wanted to give Cantro fair notice of his intentions toward Alice, but it had come within a split second of a gun fight. Cantro's jealous temper could spark and explode with the suddenness of dynamite. It still might erupt.

95

Breck abruptly veered off toward Doc Vance's office. The boxlike waiting room was vacant but he heard the faint sounds that meant a patient in the inner office. He walked to the window and looked out on the street, shifting to see the distant sheriff's office. Later on, he'd see Alice, tell her what had happened and assure her that he could wait out Frank's anger.

He frowned, thinking of Cantro's anger. Breck suddenly thought of Hallie Yates and wondered if Cantro's jealousy actually stemmed from love of Alice. How could it, with his name still associated with Hallie? It occurred to him that there might be another side of the coin, that Hallie's encouragement might stem from her knowledge that she had lost Cantro's love.

Breck sighed. Either way, Cantro's temper was real and deadly. If he had a chance to cool down, he might see that gunplay was no way to settle rivalry over Alice. Breck didn't like the idea of avoiding any man, but, in this case, it might be wise.

There were more people involved than himself and Alice. If there had been a fight a few moments ago and Cantro had killed him, what would happen to Unger, Vance, Dean an the others? If Cantro had died, what would Jerry Hecker do?

He suddenly leaned forward as he saw Frank leave the sheriff's office. The old man hurried back toward his store, throwing a frightened glance toward the Thunder. In a moment, Cantro came out. The lawman hitched at his gun belt and slowly crossed the street to the saloon. He disappeared inside.

Breck waited, watching. He had no doubt that Cantro, still anger-spurred, hunted him out, expecting him to be at the saloon. Minutes dragged by. A lift of voices brought Breck's attention to the inner office, but they subsided. He looked at the street again.

Cantro reappeared. He stood at the edge of the saloon porch and looked up and down the street, slowly, carefully. He tightened his holster to his hip and walked away, heading toward the next corner. He was soon beyond Breck's vision. Breck stepped to the door and went out on the walk. He was just in time to see Cantro turn a far corner and he knew Cantro hurried to Dane's home.

Breck had an impulse to hurry after him, but then realized that he would only add to Alice's trouble. Cantro might be angry, but he would not harm her, and it would be best for him to hear the truth from her lips. Breck's presence would only inflame the man the more. He reluctantly turned back to Doc's office.

A few moments later, the inner door opened and the patient left. Doc's face lightened when he saw Breck. "Well, now! Looks like you need a prescription. Come right in."

Breck entered the inner sanctum—a more spacious room, but crowded with a desk, medical couch, cabinets, skeleton in a corner and ancient and new textbooks on the healing art. Doc Vance opened a cabinet and pulled out a decanter, took shot glasses from a desk drawer. He poured drinks, handed one to Breck and then sat down in his creaking office chair.

"Your health!" He downed the drink and then knitted shaggy brows as he looked sharply at Breck. "From the sour look of you, I diagnose trouble."

"Some. Frank Dane and I had an argument. I told him I'd marry Alice no matter what he thought."

"So you're taking my advice. Good for you!"

"I told Cantro, too. We came close to gunplay."

Doc rubbed his thumb along his jaw, thoughtfully. "It's bound to come sooner or later. He's hell-bent to get Dane's money."

"I'd say it was jealousy."

"Maybe, Breck. You're like Jim, always seeing the best in the other man. Cantro figures Alice could do him a lot of good in San Alma so he won't let anyone move in. He's not in love with her, I'll bet you."

Breck didn't argue. Doc Vance continued after a moment. "A showdown with Cantro won't do us any good right now."

"I know. I want him to cool off. In a way, I feel like I'm running and I don't like it."

"Give yourself credit for brains. There'll be a time and a place, but *you'll* be the one who'll decide that. It'll make you feel better to know what Dean told me yesterday. Matt's working fast, and so are the others. Decent folk all over the county are willing to back us. For the first time in years, they hope someone can get 'em out from under outlaw rule."

"Now that *is* news!"

"No word's leaked yet. But we got to be careful, Breck. Like now. You're right in letting Cantro cool off. Better make sure he does."

Breck's brows rose. "You mean—"

"Don't let him run into you around town. A lot of things depend on that."

Breck sighed and slowly stood up, showing his distaste for Doc's suggestion but knowing its wisdom. The old man impishly looked up at him from under shaggy brows. "Now don't go thinking me or anyone else won't understand. I give you title here and now to Cantro's hide—at the appropriate time."

Breck grinned wryly and left. Outside, he looked toward the sheriff's office. Cantro was not in sight. Breck went to the Thunder and found Tip at the bar. Chuck and Lew had gone to the store to buy some small items.

"Cantro was here," Tip said, "looking mean as hell."

"Did he say anything?"

"Asked if you'd been around and acted like he wanted to start a fight. I just pulled in horns and said nothing, but it wasn't easy. You and him tangle?"

"In a way."

"Too bad you didn't finish it," Tip growled.

"Another time. Right now, I'm riding back to the ranch. You and the boys stay as long as you want."

"Nothing to hold me here. I'll go with you."

"Tip, you've earned your drinks and your fun. Besides, you should keep an eye on Chuck and Lew. I'll look for you tomorrow."

He pushed back from the bar, but Tip checked him, troubled. "You running from Cantro?"

"You know better." Breck had to choke back the urge to tell Tip the whole story. "He's mad at me because of Alice. You know what talk a fight over her would cause."

Tip nodded slowly. "You're right. You've got more brains —and guts—than I have. I should've known better. See you later, then."

Breck smiled tightly and walked out of the saloon. He stood a moment on the porch, looking up and down the street, feeling the impulse to stay and have it out. He fought it down, mounted his horse and turned into the increasingly heavy traffic of the street. He rode at a slow pace, half hoping to meet Cantro. It made him feel better. Nor did he ride any faster once he was clear of the town and out on the open range.

He arrived at the ranch around noon and, after a scant, tasteless meal, busied himself with small tasks about the yard. Several times he caught himself looking toward San Alma, wanting to ride back there. He wanted to see Alice, but choked down that desire. She would know what had happened by now and he was sure she would understand. She liked things clear and in the open, just as he did.

He thought of that tense moment with Cantro, broken by Frank Dane's hurried entrance. It was hard not to regret the lost chance of a showdown, but he knew that he had acted wisely, much as it galled him.

The sun was low in the west when he turned back to the house. He was hungry, but not in the mood to eat. The day had dragged by and his constant irritation and churning thoughts had made him as weary as if he had labored hard. He sighed and looked toward the road.

Tip came riding into the yard, slouched in the saddle. Breck met him at the corral. He spoke sharply. "Trouble in town?"

"Nope." The old man swung out of the saddle.

"Then what brought you back? Where's Chuck and Lew?"

"They still have a heap of drinking to do. I figured there was no point in stopping them."

"I asked you to keep an eye on them."

Tip off-saddled unconcernedly. "San Alma's real peaceful. Haven't seen the sheriff since late afternoon. I heard him and Frank Dane have been holding powwows in the store. I brought the boys' guns along, so they won't be shooting out lamps, and they've got a room at the hotel. Nothing to worry about in town."

"Then why didn't you stay?"

Tip slapped the horse's rump and it trotted into the corral. He closed the gate and faced Breck. "I just plain got tired of sitting in the Thunder and walking up and down the street. Got tired of listening to the same old talk."

"And that's all?"

"No. One other thing. I got tired of the Thunder's liquor and figured I might as well drink at home, real handy to my bunk when I got sleepy."

"We've got the same brand and you know it."

"Sure, but—somehow it tastes better."

"Tip, you're a damned old liar! But come on to the house. We'll have some of that liquor and I was about to fix supper."

"And I thought of the vittles, too," Tip added solemnly. "Heap better than San Alma's hash house."

Breck punched him lightly on the arm and they turned to the house. Breck knew that Tip had returned to the ranch in case of trouble that he didn't want Breck to face alone. But the old man knew Breck would resent this protection and so he had paraded that series of lame excuses.

They had their drinks and prepared the supper. After the meal, they moved out on the porch, taking the bottle and glasses with them. They sat there in comfortable companionship, watching the twilight deepen into night.

Tip, mellowed, spoke of Jim Malone, and Breck's uncle came alive in the quiet flow of words. Breck listened, eyes on the bright stars, and it was driven home to him that Circle M was worth all the struggle. Not only for the sake of Jim's memory, but for Alice. After the time of gunsmoke that was to come, Breck would bring her here and life would then have solid meaning and content. But before his dreams

99

could come true, he must bring peace to the whole of San Alma. No man could stand alone and isolated, for one man's violent death from an outlaw gun forecast the destruction of all. Additional steel came into Breck's determination as he listened to Tip.

Many hours passed in talk and the peace of the night made them drowsy. Tip poured a final drink and they lingered over it, chairs tipped back against the wall. Breck heard a faint sound and, at the same instant, Tip's chair banged to the floor and he came to his feet.

He spoke in a low, alarmed voice. "Someone's coming."

"I heard it."

The sound came again. Breck touched Tip's arm. "Coming through the gate now. Sounds like one man, but we'd better make sure."

Silently, they stepped off the porch, each man drawing his Colt, holding it ready. They ghosted out into the yard as the muffled beat of hoofs grew more pronounced.

"Hey, the house! Anybody home? This is Matt Unger."

Breck holstered his gun. "Ride in, Matt!"

A moment later, the looming dark shape of horse and rider appeared. Matt swung out of the saddle, ground-tied the horse. "Heard you'd left town, Breck. I figured you'd be here."

"Come up to the house. We've been jawing on the porch."

"Can't stay long if I'm to get home before midnight, Breck. Went into town late this afternoon. Talked to Doc."

"Trouble there?" Breck asked sharply.

"Not yet. Doc told me about you and Alice. I sure wish you luck. She's a mighty fine girl."

"Thanks. What about Cantro?"

Unger's chuckle held no real mirth. "Haven't seen too much of him. He's walking around like a bear with the toothache, wanting to take it out on someone. Happened to meet the gent who lives next door to Frank Dane. He said Cantro showed up looking mad and was there for a spell. He came out looking madder, if that's possible."

So Alice had made things doubly clear to Cantro, Breck thought. Unger read his thoughts. "Our sheriff was sure unhappy. He blames you."

"I know. Maybe I should've had it out."

"No, Doc is right. No use rushing something that'll come in its own good time, anyhow." He studied his glass and glanced at Tip and then at Breck, a silent signal that Breck instantly understood.

"Matt, come in the office. I want to make a dicker with you."

Tip yawned. "A night like this for business! More for

courting or sleeping, I'd say, and I'm clean beyond the age when a girl'd look twice at me. So I'm turning in. Night, Breck . . . Matt."

They listened to his fading steps and caught the distant gleam of a light from the bunkhouse as Tip struck a match. It vanished as he closed the door.

Matt cleared his throat. "I dropped in the bank this afternoon. John told me some news I think you ought to hear."

"Something gone wrong with our plans?"

"No, not yet. By the way, I told Doc today I'd prod things along a lot faster now that you and Cantro might lock horns."

"What's the news?" Breck insisted.

Matt was silent a moment. "It's about Frank Dane."

"What about him?"

"Doc says he told you some folks are suspicious of Frank, think he has some sort of deal with Jerry Hecker."

"He told me," Breck agreed.

"Well, looks like there's proof."

"What?"

"It's this way. Jed Hanlon drives the stagecoach to railhead over at Dimas. He carries the mail and small packages for folks in San Alma. Every now and then he'd take a few small boxes for Frank."

"He's a merchant. Nothing surprising."

"Except Jed noticed that he always sent them after the Hecker gang come back from one of its trips. The packages were always sent to someone in Denver—and Frank don't buy store stock that far away. Never got anything from there, just sent things out. Jed got so curious he finally hinted about 'em. Frank said it was patent medicine he sent to an old friend who couldn't get the stuff around Denver. That sounded reasonable and Jed didn't think any more about it."

"How does John Dean come in?"

"Jed carries a lot of stuff for the bank. He'd told John about those Denver packets." Matt's voice grew heavier. "Not long ago, the banker in Dimas had business with John, mostly by letter, and he mentioned Frank Dane. Said he was glad Frank steadily deposited money in his bank but wondered why John wasn't getting it. That made John curious for he knew damn well he was getting all the money from Frank's store and his interests around San Alma."

Breck said nothing.

"John wrote back. He found out Frank rode over there and picked up mail. He'd make a deposit at the bank and they wouldn't see him for a while. Then he'd show up again." Matt paused. "Always not long after he sent patent medicine

101

to Denver. He told folks around here that he was checking on the ranch he leases south of town."

"The opposite direction from Dimas," Breck said heavily.

"Going and coming, he'd ride through the Thunders. John wondered if this thing in Dimas had anything to do with the gent in Denver, so he wrote to a banker there. Claimed someone here gave the gent's name as a reference. The answer came a few days ago."

Breck braced himself. "And?"

"Turns out to be a jeweler, a real shady character. Been in trouble with the law several times. The Denver bank said to have nothing to do with whoever gave his name. He's been known to sell stolen goods for crooks, not only in Denver, but several other places."

"A fence," Breck said.

"John told Doc Vance about it. They waited and then, just this morning, Dane brings a couple more packets to Jed." Matt broke off a moment, then spoke flatly. "Jerry Hecker ain't long back from one of his trips."

Breck stood up. "I think I can guess the rest."

"That's right. John and Doc opened them packets real careful. Lucky for us they don't go through the post office. There were rings, watch charms set with stones, some jewels. It wasn't new stuff, either."

Breck walked to the edge of the porch and stared out into the night. Behind him, Matt stirred, then came up beside him. The rancher looked up toward the stars and sighed.

"Can't be nothing but stuff Hecker's taken in those holdups and robberies. He passes them on to Frank who sends them to this gent in Denver."

"The jeweler sells or buys them," Breck finished harshly, "and sends the money to Dimas, where Dane picks it up. That has to be the money he banks over there."

"And somehow he splits with Jerry," Matt added. "Frank was always one to grab a loose dollar, but, for all that, folks liked him. Brought up Alice a real lady after her mother died. You wouldn't believe this of him—but there it is."

Breck's voice choked. "I know Alice has no idea of this."

"None. You can bet once Frank did the first job for Hecker, he was trapped in all the others. They send men to jail for a long time for things like that. I'll bet that's why he's afraid Alice has turned down Cantro."

"What can be done?"

Unger sighed deeply. "Dead certain we can't go to Cantro. We'll have to wait until you're sheriff and . . ."

After a moment he said, "A hell of a thing for you to start with."

Chapter XIV

BRECK HARDLY SLEPT that night. The evidence against Frank Dane was not complete, but it was obvious that Hecker had passed stolen articles to him. Who would suspect an honest businessman and long-time resident? It was equally obvious that Dane later gave the proceeds of the sale to Hecker, undoubtedly keeping part of it for his own trouble.

Through a nearly sleepless night and most of Sunday, Breck tried to find the reason for Frank's actions.

Eagerness to amass money was part of it, as Unger believed. But there was more, and Breck finally thought he had the answer. Mrs. Dane had died some time before Breck started his wanderings. Frank had taken her death hard, had almost sickened and died of grief. Then he had recovered, and Breck guessed that this was because he'd feared to leave Alice orphaned completely.

Grieved and lonely, Frank Dane must have turned to his business, throwing himself into it to dull the pain of his loss. Looking back now, Breck could see little signs of what was to come, though Frank had been pleasant and friendly enough. Since that time, he must have become more and more immersed in the making of money until it became an obsession.

This didn't quite tie in with his undoubted love for Alice. Yet, in a way, it did. Only the need to protect her had brought Frank back from the grave. Afterward, there was the need to amass an estate so that Frank's death would assure her financial security, no matter what happened.

Something like this was the only answer Breck could find. Yet, foremost, was the terrible question of what he would do should he wear the star and have to arrest Frank. It would be even worse if he and Alice were married. What would she do?

He wanted to ride to San Alma to talk to her—not of this, of course, for she probably knew nothing about it. But he had the tortured idea that he might be able to pose the problem in an impersonal way—like, "What if I were forced to do something that might hurt you." He rejected that, but the need to just see her still remained.

Late Sunday afternoon, Chuck and Lew came riding in,

still showing faint signs of a morning of remorse after an all-night fight with the Thunder's liquor. Between their physical discomfort and Breck's mental turmoil, the Circle M had a decided air of gloom. Breck was glad to get into bed and blow out the lamp. It seemed as though the act cut out the world and its problems.

But they remained with him in the darkness and pounced on him the moment he opened his eyes the next morning. Breck hurried to saddle a horse and ride off toward San Alma. He held to a steady, mile-eating pace and it was not long before he saw, far ahead, the first scattering of houses at the edge of town.

He drew rein and grimly checked his gun, then slipped it back into the holster and considered what his immediate steps should be. He knew that Frank Dane would be at the store and Alice probably at home. This suited Breck, for he wanted to avoid Frank and he didn't want to run into Cantro.

With a bitter dislike for the necessity of avoiding trouble, Breck reined off the road and started a slow circle of the town to drift in where he would have a short ride down the side street to Alice's house.

He had little fear of meeting Cantro out here, so he allowed his tumultuous thoughts to engulf him and was hardly aware that he was approaching a neat, isolated cottage.

There was a flicker of movement at white lace curtains over a big front window, but Breck's eyes now cast ahead along the road that became a street some distance away. It rolled northward toward the Thunder range and between the houses in the opposite direction. He angled across it, now very close to the small house on his left. The door opened and Breck's hand instantly dropped to his holster.

Hallie Yates, just within the door, beckoned to him. "Mr. Malone! I want to talk to you."

He reined in, gray eyes cutting sharply to the window, then beyond the house. She read his suspicion. "I'm alone. Tie your horse beyond the barn where it won't be seen."

Breck sat a moment, frowning, puzzled. Then he gave a nod and turned toward the small barn beyond the house. As he circled the cottage, he studied each window, his hand never far from his gun. There was no movement, no challenge.

He left his horse ground-tied in the shelter of the barn. He stood at its corner, looking toward the house, eyes casting to the road and the bushes that lined the yard. The back door opened and Hallie stepped into full view.

"Please, Mr. Malone. I think we ought to talk."

He moved clear of the barn then and crossed the yard.

She was waiting for him just inside the door. He entered a small kitchen, still tense and suspicious. A hall led to the front of the house. Windows admitted sunlight in a broad square across the scrubbed wooden top of the table and the clean floor, touched the highly polished black stove. There were chairs around the table and Hallie sat down in one, indicating another. Breck swept off his hat and sat down, ears straining for any small sound that would indicate a trap.

"There's no one here," she said and studied her hands, folded on the table top. Breck waited. She looked up, her dark eyes moving away from his, then returning.

"It's about Alice Dane," she blurted.

His voice had an edge. "What about her?"

"I . . . know what's between you and Roy. I'll do what I can to help you."

He studied her a moment. "I can understand why."

Her eyes did not waver. "Then you *do* know about Roy and me. There's been talk, lots of it."

"Enough." His voice became gentle. "But could you expect anything else?"

"No . . . not really. Then you understand that if you marry her, you'll be doing me a favor."

"Cantro will do everything he can to stop me."

Her face clouded. "I know Roy. I should, after all these years. You're hinting there might be trouble—gun trouble. I think I can prevent a bullet showdown."

"It's a gamble," Breck warned.

"What else can I do? See him married to her?"

Breck's eyes softened. "Does he know how much you're in love with him?"

She made a small, hopeless gesture. "I don't know. Sometimes I think he does. But one thing I know—I love him."

"How did it happen?"

"Years ago, down in Arizona." Her dark eyes lifted and Breck saw that she wanted to talk, to express her feelings to someone who would not be likely to take it to Cantro. He waited, letting her make the decision to speak or be silent.

"I haven't always been a seamstress," she said in a low voice. "I've been in the dancehalls, dealt faro, drifted—ever since my folks died."

Her first words came out with difficulty, forced. Then she spoke with greater freedom and Breck listened, his understanding and sympathy mounting.

Orphaned by an Apache raid from which she had miraculously escaped, Hallie had faced a harsh, pitiless world without friends or money. She had turned in desperation to one of the few means of making a living open to a lovely girl in the sun-blasted, far-scattered towns of the southwest.

She had drifted from one place to another, managing always to keep intact a deep, solid core of self-respect. Time and again this loyalty to self had lost her jobs, sent her drifting again. She'd landed in a small town not far from Nogales. By then, she was bone-weary of life, asking herself why she bothered to fight any longer.

She met Roy Cantro, a deputy already showing the qualities that would later make his reputation as a lawman along the border. She sighed now as she told Breck about it. "There was something we saw in one another—a sort of honesty or code. I knew Roy had it then and, because of it, he understood what I had to fight."

So friendship grew. Roy gave her a new courage and soon it became apparent to the habituées of the saloon where she dealt faro that he was her unofficial protector. An insult, hint or innuendo meant a quick and unpleasant call from the young deputy. Hallie, for her part, fostered Roy's ambitions, counseled patience until the right law job came along.

"We were in love," she told Breck. "But Roy had no job for a married man. It paid just enough, in that little place, for him to get by until a better job came along. So I kept on at the saloon, knowing it would all work out. I was willing to wait."

Then came a series of deputy jobs, forcing Roy to move from place to place. Hallie moved with him, seeing in each new job an upward step, a building of his reputation.

"But it did mine no good," she added with weary bitterness. "We still had to wait until Roy became a full sheriff or marshal somewhere. We decided maybe I'd best leave the faro games and dancehalls. I always had a knack with a needle and so I became a seamstress. More respectable, Roy said, and I felt that way, too."

She fell silent again. Breck waited, his understanding deepening with his pity. But he knew he dared not show it, for Hallie still had pride. Only love for Roy Cantro had caused any diminishing of it.

She broke the silence, saying that Roy had finally become a sheriff and she knew then that things would be changed. But they didn't, and she couldn't quite understand why. Roy gave her sound arguments about low pay, about towns being reluctant to hire a lawman with a wife unless he had a real big name.

"That was true of Tres Cruces," she said. "Some said it was plain suicide to wear a law badge there. They believed

106

a man with a wife would move too easily and carefully, and Tres Cruces needed a man with fast guns and guts. Roy had those, and they didn't know about me. He cleaned up the place."

"I know." Breck nodded.

"I never knew in the morning if he'd be alive at sundown. Then came the offer from San Alma. Deputy under Jip Terry. It paid as much as Tres Cruces, but Roy didn't want to be a deputy again. I persuaded him to take it. It was peaceful compared to Tres Cruces and it was sort of agreed Roy would step into Jip's shoes when the old man retired. All that has happened. Roy is exactly where he wants to be."

Her short laugh was dry and bitter. "But I still take in sewing on the edge of town. Roy likes it here and wants to stay. I'd like it, too, if I knew things would change for me. I'm as much in love with him as I ever was and I thought he felt the same toward me. Now I know better. There's Alice Dane. Roy has all kinds of good arguments, but it adds up to the fact that I'm not good enough for him. I don't have a wealthy father. I'm not the kind of woman the sheriff of San Alma should marry!"

Her eyes blazed. "There was nothing I could do about it. But now you've come. You've upset his plans and I'll do all I can to keep them upset."

"What?"

Her lips thinned. "I don't know yet; depends on how things develop. But I did want you to know how I feel."

He leaned forward, eyes and voice sharp. "Like I said, this could lead to trouble."

"I have to take the chance," she said in a low voice. "If Roy is killed, I don't know what I would do. But, on the other hand, how can I go on this way? What will happen to me if he marries Alice Dane? I think I still have enough influence with Roy to make him see reason. A fight with you over the girl will harm him, even if he wins. Given time, I can make him see that."

"I hope so," Breck said gravely.

"But walk careful," she said sharply. "Roy is fast with a gun. I hate to say it of him, but he can be mean and tricky when he gets mad, like he is now."

"I'll watch him."

"And his friends, too. They can be even worse."

"The Hecker gang?"

Abruptly, she stood up and Breck slowly rose, the question still between them. "I don't know all his friends," she evaded, "but I know what some of them are like. I want you to stay alive to marry Alice Dane."

Suddenly her eyes lighted and she leaned toward him. "Does she love you, Mr. Malone?"

"Yes."

"Then go to her. Persuade her to elope with you. Marry her and ride out. Stay out of town."

"Stay?" he exclaimed.

"Roy would never forget a thing like that. I know him. If you came back, he'd find some way to even the score, to make him feel he got the best of you, after all. He'll be sheriff here as long as he likes. There's no chance of him losing an election so long as—" She caught herself. "He'd kill you, or make life miserable for you. A sheriff has many ways to cripple a man besides a bullet. And his friends— they could bushwhack you without warning."

Breck shook his head. "I'm trying to persuade Alice to marry me right away. But to leave town and stay away— no, I couldn't do that."

She came close in her excitement. "But it's the answer for both of us, don't you see? If you need money until you could settle things here—"

"No, Hallie. It'll work out. We'll both do what we can. I'm glad to know how you feel, and thanks for telling me."

Disappointment showed clearly in her face. "Please, Mr. Malone. Marry her right away."

"I aim to ask her now. That's where I was heading."

He left the house, throwing a quick glance along the road. In a few moments, he rode away from the cottage, heading directly toward Alice Dane's home.

He felt a new surge of confidence. Not that he could clearly see how Hallie could help, but the fact that she was his ally—so far as Alice was concerned—lessened the odds with Cantro. At least she would act as a brake on Roy, and this was a help until such time as Unger would give the signal for open war.

He regretted that he could not have asked her what had changed Roy, but too much interest in him as a lawman might have aroused Hallie's suspicions. Despite her offer to help with Alice, Breck knew she would protect Cantro in every other way.

Breck came to Alice's street and, caution still riding him, turned along the narrow path behind the houses. He knocked on the kitchen door, heard an immediate stir. Alice took one startled look at him and then threw herself in his arms. A moment later, she pulled him inside, fear touching her eyes.

"Breck, you shouldn't be here!"

"I have to see you. I have to know what's happened."

She gave him a tremulous smile. "It's been pretty awful, but I don't mind so long as its for us."

"Your father?"

"He's furious, but at least I can argue with him. I think deep down under he wants me to be happy but doesn't want to admit that you're the one I should marry. He sounds like he won't give in, but I think eventually he will. Father doesn't worry me so much as Roy."

"You've told him?"

"Over and over. He won't listen, Breck. He swears he'll kill you if he sees you in town. I'm afraid he'll try it." She came to him, held him close. "I'm frightened. Roy means what he says."

He worked his fingers under her chin and lifted her face so she looked directly into his eyes. His voice was soft. "So do I, Alice. We can end all of this, fast. Say the word and we'll ride off to the nearest town and get married."

"Breck, I want to . . . oh, so badly. But it won't end this thing, at least not with Roy."

"What could he do?"

"Make me a widow," she answered simply. She held tightly to his arms. "Can't you see that if I hold fast, there's nothing Dad or Roy can do? Patience—that's the only answer."

"No time," Breck said shortly.

"But there is. Believe me, darling!"

He strode to the door and looked blindly out on the yard. He wished he could tell her that they were already close to a showdown and that her father might be ruined in the explosion that was bound to come. He felt trapped, and it flashed into his mind that he should tell Matt and Doc he would not run for sheriff. But if he did, San Alma would be more firmly under outlaw rule. On the other hand, as sheriff, he faced the problem with Frank Dane.

Alice came up behind him and slowly turned him about. She kissed him again. "Please, Breck? I think it's best if we just wait. It can't be long, and then think of all the years—"

He kissed her swiftly and savagely. Then he was out the door and striding away, seething with a futile anger. She was right, but she did not dream how. He knew she must be staring after him, puzzled, fearing he was angry. But he dared not stay another moment for fear of blurting out information.

He swung into the saddle and savagely reined the horse about. One moment he wanted to have it out with Cantro and the next he knew he should ride out and avoid conflict. One moment he decided to find Unger and call this election business off and the next moment he knew he could not break faith with desperate men and friends who depended on him.

He came to the end of the block and blindly turned toward the main road, his mind still an angry, clashing ebb and flow of thoughts. He dimly discerned the figure in the dark suit that started to turn into one of the houses, saw him and stopped short.

A harsh voice lashed at him. "Malone! What in hell are you doing in town?"

Breck's head jerked up and he looked at Doc Vance. The shaggy brows were drawn in an angry frown, the jaw and eyes hard with disapproval.

Doc stepped up to Breck's stirrup. His eyes flashed. "We asked you to stick close to Circle M."

"I had to see Alice."

Doc's jaw was still set and firm. "That's an excuse of sorts —but not enough. Cantro's roaming around and he'd like nothing better than to tangle with you."

"I'm willing!"

"I'm not. You tangle with Cantro now and you hurt everything we're trying for. Now you git! And stay put!" His voice softened. "It's not easy, Breck. I know that. But it won't be long. Don't do a foolish thing that'll hurt your friends."

Breck started to blurt that he was no longer sure he would go through with it. Then, in a flash, he knew that he could not be false to his word. There were greater problems than his own here, involving every person in the county.

His lips snapped shut and he lifted the reins. "All right, Doc—this time. But my patience is running out of rope. I wasn't made to run and hide."

"I know. But it's a near thing now. You'll have your chance to blow this county wide open—Hecker and Cantro with it! Now git before trouble walks around the corner."

Breck bleakly rode off, heading back the way he had come, to avoid any chance encounter. It rubbed him raw. More than it ever had before.

Chapter XV

THERE WERE MANY square miles of Circle M range. Enough for a man to ride out restlessness. And there was enough work to keep him occupied. But, despite daily hard riding and work, Breck felt confined to a cell.

The boundaries of the ranch were his walls and he had to fight himself to keep within them. He used every deep resource of stubbornness, duty and obligation. Every instinct called him to San Alma, and he could only grit his teeth and wait.

Even so, he came close to losing his battle when Doc Vance brought news that Alice was having a continuing battle with her father. Cantro still breathed threats in an effort to make her change her mind.

Breck listened, pacing the room. He whirled to face Doc when the old man finished. "She's fighting *my* battle!"

"She wants to, Breck. She asked me to tell you to be patient. Knowing her, I think she can handle Frank and Roy Cantro."

"But that should be up to me!"

"You've told him you want to marry her and he won't give his consent. Now it's only proper that she persuade him. What more can you do?"

Breck's face planed into ugly lines. "I could stop Cantro, that's certain."

"And let the rest of us down?"

"Damn it! I—" He broke off short. Doc Vance watched him, knowingly. Breck came close to irrevocably turning his back on his friends. Some inner strength—something he could not quite define—stopped him. He slapped his fist into his palm. "It's a hell of a mess, whatever I do!"

"Point is, do you want to face it?"

Doc met Breck's scrutiny, his own level eyes a challenge. Breck's face softened. "You understand what's pulling me, don't you?"

"Yes. But I can't help you. Wouldn't if I could. It's your decision and you live with it."

"I won't go back on what I promised you, Doc."

"I never once thought you would."

"Then you have more faith in me than I've got!"

"You're wrong there, Breck. A man with no faith in himself and his word wouldn't act as you have. You've fought out a decision. You're stronger because of it."

Breck grinned crookedly. "You're preaching, Doc. Trying to make me feel good."

"Not preaching. Just saying what I feel and know." He stood up, sighed. "Got to get along. Sit tight and hold fast. It won't be long."

Out in the yard, Breck checked the old man as he started to drive away. "You'll see Alice?"

"Of course! Figured you'd have a message for her."

"Just . . . tell her I haven't changed. It's hard to stay here knowing what she's facing. But I will. Tell her that."

Doc nodded, slapped the reins on the horse's rump, and the old buggy rattled out of the yard.

Breck found new reservoirs of patience after Doc's visit and, for a few days, was able to bury himself in work and the ranch. He hoped for word each day, but none came. Then he felt a renewed stirring of his restlessness and impatience.

Finally Matt Unger came, refused to dismount, but grinned in triumph at Breck. "We're ready."

"When?"

"We have the signature sheets supporting you as candidate for office. We could tip our hand now, but it's best to show strength the day you file. There'll be a heap of friends riding with you then."

"Will we need them?"

Matt's face grew tight. "They have to know you've got guns to back you or Hecker will figure, sure as hell, a dead candidate is no candidate at all."

Breck felt excitement rise and his gray eyes sparked. "Where will we meet?"

"Mostly in town, but some of the boys will be at my place and we'll ride in with you. Have your own crew ready. We'll have a meeting the night before to make final plans."

"Have it here," Breck suggested.

"Why not? No need to skip around in shadows any more. See you Monday night, then, and Tuesday morning we break San Alma wide open."

Those last few days were the worst time of all, relieved only when Breck called in his crew the night following Matt's visit. Breck served drinks and then told them of the plan to break the outlaw grip on the county. They stared in stunned surprise and then their faces lighted with pleased grins. Tip slapped his thigh when Breck finished.

112

"I could figure you'd work something like this! It's sure good news."

"Where do we fit in?" Chuck asked.

"That's up to you. We all know what this move will mean —bullets. So I want each of you to decide. This is one time I won't give orders."

"I'm throwing in!" Tip exclaimed.

Lew laughed. "You just tell me what you want done."

"That goes for me," Chuck added.

Breck smiled. "That makes it perfect. We're still a crew."

On Saturday, Breck decided it was best to stay close to the ranch. He had an almost superstitious feeling that the slightest thing could upset the whole plan, now that they were this close to action. So he and the boys loafed about the yard. Breck could not keep his eyes from the gate, half expecting a rider with further news. If the plan went according to schedule, even now riders from all over the county would be converging on San Alma or gathering at Matt Unger's. But nothing marred the dull peace of the week end. Monday passed in nervous inactivity.

But just at supper time, Doc Vance's buggy rattled into the yard. Breck hurried out to meet him.

"Can you spare feed for an old nag and an old goat?" Doc asked. "I reckon both of us will be here a time."

The horse was turned into a stall and Doc ate with Breck and the crew. He had a few private words with Breck—news that Alice still withstood a kind of seige and sent her love. He expressed pleasure that Tip, Chuck and Lew made three more guns to count on.

Matt Unger showed up after dark, Lashlee and Sears with him. Then John Dean rode in. Breck brought them into the main room of the ranch house, then posted Tip and the men out in the dark yard to keep watch.

Breck returned to the house and faced the men gathered there. John Dean spoke quietly. "Well, Breck, starting tomorrow you become a target."

"I'll try to be hard to hit. What's the plan?"

"There's a bunch at my place, waiting back in that canyon," Unger answered. "We'll be here a little after sunup. You'll be ready by then?"

"I'm ready now, for that matter. Will there be trouble in town?"

Doc Vance chuckled. "Not as much as we thought."

"The outlaws seem to be out on one of their jobs somewhere," Dean said. "Generally they don't return for several days."

113

"Then Cantro's alone," Breck cut in.

"That's right. By now, he's probably wondering why so many down-county ranchers and riders are drifting into town. Come morning, he'll get the answer, but he won't be able to do much about it."

Sears spoke up. "Half of Riata's there—or will be."

"A dozen from my end of the county," Lashlee added.

"Some from the north," Unger tallied and grinned tightly. "It'll be a big day."

"Then we'd better get some rest," Doc Vance said flatly. He looked around sharply. "No change in plans? Everyone understands what he has to do?"

Matt growled deep in his throat. "How could we forget something we've been working for all this time? Breck, be ready to ride when I show up. Lashlee, you'll be in town. Keep an eye on the courthouse when we ride in."

The young rancher grinned and nodded. They shook hands with Breck and soon he stood on the dark porch listening to the fading beat of their horses as they rode away.

Tip drifted in, stood beside him, listening. "Sheriff Breck Malone. Jim'd sure be proud and I wonder what Jip Terry would say about it?"

"He'd wonder what made me think I could wear a badge."

"Jip was no fool, Breck. He always said you had the makings of a man, even when you was at your wildest. Well, I reckon you'll prove that in the next few months."

Breck was up before dawn. By the time the eastern tips of the Granadas showed the first gray light, he was out in the corral and saddling up. He checked his gun, his ammunition and pushed a rifle into the saddle scabbard.

Tip, Lew and Chuck grimly prepared for the day and then the four of them squatted by the corral gate to await the coming of Matt Unger. Breck saw the rise of dust on the road leading to the ranch. Without a word, the four men swung into saddle and rode out of the yard just as Unger and more than a dozen men appeared.

Unger's sharp eyes touched Breck's holster and the rifle protruding from the scabbard, then lifted to Breck's face, searching and weighing. His face cleared and his lips moved in a slight smile.

"Let's git you started for sheriff," he said shortly and swung his horse around. Breck fell in beside him and the cavalcade started for San Alma. They rode at an easy but steady gait, speaking little, feeling the early-morning chill and the gravity of the mission on which they rode.

They were near Running W when another group of riders

swung in to meet them. Then once more they lined out for San Alma at a steady pace.

Their pace did not slacken as they approached the town, but here and there a man loosened a gun in the holster or rubbed his right palm along his trouser leg to make sure sweat would not interfere with a quick, certain draw.

Unger, without changing pace, stood in the stirrups and twisted about. His steady voice carried clearly. "Keep your heads. Make no move for a gun unless Breck or I do. We'll avoid a fight if we can, but we ain't backing down. If trouble comes, I expect it at the courthouse, but be ready for it at any time."

He looked at Breck. "From now on, you're in charge. We follow your lead. Whatever it takes for you to wear the law badge, do it, and we won't ask questions."

"You're putting a lot of faith in me."

"That's right. If we didn't think you were worth it, you wouldn't be riding with us now."

Unger rode on, jaw rock-hard. Breck felt the overwhelming force of the faith these men had in him, and it left him humble, in a sense, and determined to justify it. He caught Tip's sharp eye and the old man slowly nodded as though Breck had spoken aloud a pledge and a promise.

Even at this early hour, there was an unusual stir in town. Several times Breck saw half-frightened faces in windows and open doorways watching the grim procession pass. Now and then a man would leave one of the houses, gun belt snugged to his waist, hat pulled low, jaw hard. Soon the horsemen were trailed by nearly twenty armed men walking in the street behind them.

As they came into the courthouse square, Breck saw Lashlee, Sears and Doc Vance heading another large group moving in from the far side. Breck stared in honest surprise, wondering if every male citizen of the county had appeared to support him. It was ridiculous, he thought, but the size of the crowd was staggering.

Breck rode to one of the many hitchracks before the courthouse and looked toward the building. The solid doors were closed and there was no one about. Unger came up beside him, pulled a big watch from his pocket and replaced it.

"We're a little early for the county clerk." He looked around the rapidly filling square. "But I reckon news of this crowd will bring him in a hurry."

"Or scare him off."

"Then we'll just have to go get him," Unger answered evenly.

115

Doc Vance, Lashlee and Sears came up as Breck and Matt dismounted. The rest of the cavalcade wheeled into the other racks, tied their mounts and then drifted in toward Breck. John Dean pushed through the crowd and Breck saw that he, too, wore a gun.

He smiled. "We turned out quite a party for you."

Breck, awed, shook his head. "All these for me?"

"Most of 'em—and I have their signatures for your filing petition." Dean pulled a thick roll of papers from his pocket and briefly displayed page on page of scrawled names. "These will be attached to the regular filing form. There are more than enough names to put you on the ballot, so the clerk has to accept it."

There was a flurry in the crowd, a continuous parting and closing from the far side of the square, like water giving way to an object and coalescing again as it passed. Suddenly men were forcibly pushed aside and Cantro stepped into the cleared space before Breck.

The sheriff was disheveled, his hat awry, black eyes flashing in anger, pale face set. He pulled up short when he saw Breck and his lips curled disdainfully. "I can sure expect *you* to be at the bottom of any trouble."

"No trouble, Sheriff," Breck answered easily.

Cantro's eyes flicked to the crowd, then back to Breck in disbelief. "I got another idea. All this crowd, and you're not wearing a gun just to look pretty. Break this up and ride on about your business."

"This *is* my business. I'm waiting for the County Clerk."

A voice in the crowd lifted. "He sure is!"

The crowd parted as a short, chubby man was pushed forward. He looked frightened, and his full cheeks quivered. His tie was awry and his white shirt crumpled from fighting his way through the crowd. Now, free of the press, he swayed to catch his balance and smoothed his vest.

He recovered some of his aplomb and glared at Breck like an angered cherub. "What is the meaning of this?"

"We're waiting to see you."

"It must be damned important," Cantro said with heavy sarcasm, "to bring out all this crowd. I've had enough of it. Break it up and head out."

"Not yet," Breck snapped. He looked at the clerk. "Are you ready for business?"

The man threw a glance at Cantro and gained courage from the lawman's presence. "The legal work of the county cannot be hurried, sir. My office will be open in fifteen minutes. At that time, you may transact your business."

"If he's here," Cantro said shortly.

116

Breck's cold gray eyes held the clerk. "Friend, don't you reckon you'd better open up?"

The clerk became aware of Breck's harsh face, of Matt Unger, Tip and the other armed men around him. He swallowed, turned on his heel and hurried to the courthouse.

Cantro faced Breck, lips compressed, hand close to his gun. "I've ordered you out of town, Malone."

Matt made a slight move, but Breck checked him. "Cantro, make sure what you're doing. I want to do this job peaceful if I can."

"What job?"

"I'm filing as candidate for sheriff."

Cantro's expression slowly changed—from tight anger to blank surprise. His jaw dropped as his brain tried to digest this bit of stunning news. Then his face suffused and he laughed. "You! Sheriff!"

There was a stir and angry murmur from the crowd. Cantro suddenly realized that he faced grim, serious men. His black eyes flicked from man to man, then back to Breck.

"You're wasting your time! Even if you could get enough signatures to file—"

John Dean lifted the thick bundle of pages lined with names. He spoke quietly. "I'll remind you of a few things. As sheriff, you are sworn to see each man has his right under the law. Malone wishes to legally file for an office and has the proper number of signatures. The County Clerk must accept his filing, and you have no right to interfere."

Matt Unger spoke up with a growl. "And the rest of us intend to see he files."

Cantro's eyes blazed. He stood with his hand close to his gun. Then he became aware of all the others, sensed that they waited for him to make a move. This was revolt, clear and unmistakable. For a moment, Cantro was swayed by the stunning surprise of it.

He moistened his lips and—slowly—his hand moved away from his gun. He looked directly at Breck and his lips curled, both in contempt and challenge. Just then, the courthouse doors opened and the chubby clerk threw a look at the crowd and darted back to the comparative safety of his office.

"Sheriff!" Cantro grunted. "You! All right, file. For all the good it'll do you."

He stepped aside and made a taunting, sweeping gesture, inviting Breck to go right in and waste all the time he wished. But Breck saw the faint glint of alarm and hate under the sardonic smile. Then Cantro turned and his eyes

117

moved about the square, marking this man and that, as though for later attention. None looked away or seemed to be frightened.

Cantro turned back to Breck. "How many will vote for you come election day?"

"Now *you're* wasting your time," Breck answered. "Point is, where do *you* stand?"

He turned to the courthouse, Matt and John Dean flanking him, Lashlee, Sears and the others falling in behind, ignoring Cantro. As Breck mounted the steps, he caught a glimpse of Frank Dane's worried face. The merchant pushed back into the crowd as Breck walked into the narrow, musty hall.

The clerk stood behind the barrier of the heavy counter. His cherubic face was drawn and he nervously rubbed his hands together as the group pushed into the narrow office space.

He moistened his lips. "Now, Mr. Malone, what can I do for you?"

"I'm filing for the office of sheriff."

"And here are twice the required number of voter signatures," Dean placed the sheets before him.

The clerk's jaw dropped. He looked around until he saw Cantro, who had pushed his way to the far end of the counter.

Breck saw the questioning look and his jaw tightened. "Do you need his permission?"

The clerk's pudgy hands made flustered movements. "I— well, no . . . but I'm surprised—"

Cantro spoke harshly. "Give him the forms, Getz. All these gents have read up real good on the law."

The clerk turned quickly and awkwardly pawed through a file. He produced the forms. There was a tense silence as Breck filled them in with a bold, black handwriting. He pushed the paper and the supporting sheaf of signatures toward the clerk.

Getz hesitated and then, swiftly, placed his official signature, stamp and date on the papers. He spoke in a choked voice. "That will do it, Mr. Malone."

Breck faced Cantro. He spoke quietly. "We lock horns."

Cantro's voice remained level. "We've already locked horns. But now you'll find out what it's like to buck something you can't handle. I promise you a fight."

He shoved men aside and strode out the door. The echo of his threat remained in the room.

Chapter XVI

THREE NIGHTS LATER, moonlight brought into bright relief the small cottage on the north edge of town. The ink-black shadows hid the saddled horses beyond the barn and a silent guard slouched on the roofed porch. The house itself was dark, except for a faint glow of light escaping from a heavy drape drawn over the window.

Within the lighted room, Hallie Yates tried hard to conceal worry and fright as Jerry Hecker paced angrily back and forth. His lips were bloodless and his face ugly. The flecked eyes looked predatory, a feral green. His very pacing reminded Hallie of a stalking panther. She fearfully watched his hand brush by his holstered Colt as he moved back and forth, fingers taloning one moment, relaxing the next.

Across the room, Frank Dane also watched the deadly pacing. The old merchant struck a false note in the group. He held himself aloof, as though only business had brought him here. He showed a faint air of disdain, persisting though he warily eyed Jerry's prowling.

Chulo Wyeth stood against the far wall, holding himself quite still, as if he knew the slightest quiver would bring Jerry's wrath blazing upon him. Chulo's muddy eyes followed his boss, threw a pitying, awed glance at Cantro and then went back again to Jerry.

Cantro sat in the big chair, lips held so tightly between his teeth that Hallie could see the red pressure line. His face was drawn and his hands had clenched into fists. But for all his anger, he kept his glittering eyes on the floor.

"A fool! You've been a fool!" Jerry flung the words contemptuously over his shoulder. Cantro flinched and his right hand slowly lifted. Hallie's breath caught in her throat for the second that his hand remained poised. Slowly she exhaled as it dropped.

Jerry whipped around and glared down at the sheriff. "You should have had some word of this long ago."

"Did you?" Cantro demanded, without looking up.

"No. And why? Because you're the one who's supposed to catch onto anything stirring and let me know. I depended on you—and a hell of a mistake that turned out to be!"

119

His blazing eyes swept over Hallie without seeing her. Jerry walked to the table, touched the whiskey bottle and then, with a gesture of angry impatience, moved back to Cantro.

"Breck Malone files for sheriff and you knew nothing about it until it was done! I can't figure where your ears or eyes were."

"How was I to know he'd do a thing like that?"

"How?" Jerry threw his hands wide in a hopeless gesture. Then his voice dropped. He spoke slowly, as though explaining something to a child. "Malone didn't decide to file just the night before, my friend. All those signatures, all that crowd—where did they come from? That meant preparation. Weeks of it. It meant Malone's friends were riding all over the county, talking to people, lining them up."

Jerry's voice lifted. "There must have been some kind of talk for you to catch."

"There was nothing."

"I'm not fool enough to believe that. There had to be a leak. But you—" Jerry glared at him. "You've been so damned anxious to get Alice Dane you couldn't see or hear anything else."

Frank Dane's head lifted and his lined face hardened. But a glance at Hecker killed his protest and he stared stonily at the far wall.

Cantro stirred. "What chance has Malone got?"

"Chance? Every chance! Are you so blind you can't see it?" Jerry's eyes narrowed in thought and he seemed to speak as much to himself as to the others. "Here's San Alma —the town and the county—the one safe place for me and the boys. Once we cross the county line, no one's going to bother us. The law works with us and gets his share." Jerry's eyes flickered venomously at Cantro. "Or at least he works when he can keep his mind off a woman."

"Let be," Cantro snapped.

"Judge Tracy does exactly as I say. We can even sell off the trinkets we pick up here and there, thanks to Frank. It took a long time to work that out, and shooting, too, until the fools learned they live with us or wear a coffin. So they left us alone—except now and then one'd need a lesson, like Jim Malone."

"That was a mistake," Frank Dane said in a low voice.

Jerry made an angry gesture. "It wouldn't have been. I gave Breck Malone rope and I planned to call taws when we came back from the jobs down south. But now this election can wipe out everything we've built."

120

Cantro finally looked up. "You're talking mad, Jerry. It's not that bad."

"I'm talking mad and I'm talking true. Damn you, Roy, for not getting on to this thing when it started. We could've blown it wide open."

"Will you quit blaming me!"

"It's no use, I reckon," Jerry growled. "The damage is done. By, by God, you'll help undo it!"

"How?" Dane asked.

Jerry walked to the table and poured himself a drink. He moved the glass around in his fingers, frowning. The rest watched him and Hallie saw the cold, swift calculation that made him so far superior to men like Chulo. She knew Roy did not have this ability to consider a problem without emotion. Jerry returned to his chair, his eyes distant, and she could almost see the quick way his brain worked.

"There's organization behind Malone. That's certain. The point is that most everyone is behind it. They see him as the one chance to throw you out, Roy."

"That'll be just the beginning," Dane said.

"Just the beginning," Jerry nodded. "There'll be no sheriff on our side and you can bet we won't have a judge. Tracy's such a drunken coward that one word from Malone will send him packing. No court for us, then, and no law. I need them both and I intend to keep them. Otherwise, every damn one of us faces a hangnoose or life in prison."

Hallie closed her eyes, a new fear for Roy welling up.

"The answer is to smash this whole thing just as fast as we can," Jerry said.

"Are you going to raid every ranch in the county?" Cantro demanded.

"I'm not that foolish. A ranch hit here and there is something the local sheriff handles. But if we start a regular war, you can bet your last dollar the governor will send in troops. We might as well let Malone win right now."

Jerry grinned wolfishly. "We strike where it counts most. There have to be three or four big ranchers backing Malone. All right, hit them, gun them down or rustle them blind. The rest will head for cover. A few gun fights in town will pick off the key figures there."

Frank Dane shuddered. "That's a cold-blooded way of doing it."

"This is a cold-blooded business. It's them or us, and you can bet every dishonest dollar you've made it'll be them."

He ignored the slow flush that mounted to Dane's cheeks. "That'll break up this thing. Find out who's really behind

121

Malone and take them out, one by one. Once Malone's all by himself, we can take him anytime we want."

Chulo stirred. "Why wait? I'd sure like to cut a notch for Malone anytime you give the word."

Jerry considered Chulo for a long moment and the big gunman's heavy face grew eager. Then the light died in his eyes as Jerry slowly shook his head.

"That tempts me, Chulo, but it's the wrong thing to do."

"I don't know," Cantro cut in. "If one of us had gunned him down before this, we wouldn't have this problem now."

"Maybe it was a mistake to handle him the way I did," Jerry admitted. "But this is not the time to kill Malone. He's a candidate for sheriff. If he dies, there'll be a stink all over the Territory. We'll take out his backers first. We'll throw bullet-fear into the county."

His eyes rested on Hallie. For the first time, he seemed to notice her as a woman, deliberately studying her body. Her cheeks flamed and she choked down a protest. Jerry's smile grew more pronounced. "Say, maybe we won't need much gunplay. Not if we could smear Malone."

"What do you mean?" Cantro asked.

Jerry still looked at Hallie. "Malone plans to marry Alice and the whole town knows about it. But suppose people find out he's tangled up with another woman? What happens to his fine reputation then?"

"But who?"

Jerry indicated Hallie. Her eyes widened in stunned protest. "Figure there's some way you could get him here, alone?"

Her look sought Cantro, certain that he would be shocked by this proposal. But Roy sat with mouth pursed, considering the plan. Instead of refusing to tolerate the suggestion, he sat there weighing its possibilities.

Hallie felt disgust and nausea. She could only look at Roy, unbelieving, her heart crying out a silent, anguished protest. She waited, certain that at any second he would protest, but he continued to stare at the rug.

Her face paled as she answered Jerry in a choked voice. "I'll not consider it. Malone's not that kind of man and I'm not that kind of person, either."

Roy's head jerked up. "She's right, Jerry. It won't work."

Hallie sank back, bitter. Roy's protest had come too late. What kind of man is he? she thought.

Jerry bit at his lip, momentarily frustrated, and then his face lighted again. "There's another way. Frank, your daughter and Malone are hell-bent on getting married. She'd fall for a fake note from him as fast as he'd fall for one from her. We could get them together in some shack or out-of-

122

the-way place. We could walk in on them and then spread the word, build it up. What would they think of the upstanding, dependable Breck Malone then?"

Dane came to his feet and Cantro sat frozen, pale face darkening. The old man caught his voice first. "You can't mean it!"

"I don't know yet. It depends on what happens when—"

"It depends on nothing!" Dane roared. "You're not using my daughter in a scheme like that."

"And I won't stand for it, either," Cantro snapped.

Hallie looked at Cantro, seeing him almost as a stranger. She felt vindictive pleasure as Jerry's lips moved contemptuously and his voice lashed at both of them.

"You'll stand for it, Cantro, if I decide on it. Dane, you'll follow orders—just like Roy"

They met his implacable eyes. He did not need to word the alternative to disobedience. Cantro swayed forward, as though to challenge him here and now. Chulo's hand moved slightly and Jerry waited, deadly and assured.

Frank Dane's eyes moved about the room as though searching for a weapon. He knew that Jerry hinted of bullet-death, if not long years in the penitentiary, because of his shipments to Denver. Cantro eased back on his heels, retreating. Dane's lined face sagged, knowing he could do nothing alone.

Jerry, knowing he had won, spoke in a lighter tone. "I haven't said we'd move that way yet. It's a good idea. Still, I'll have to think it over."

"There are other ways," Cantro growled.

"Sure—and let's look at them."

Jerry dropped into his chair, leaving the two men standing. Cantro glanced at Frank and slowly sat down. Dane stood a moment longer, knobby hands clenched, and then he too eased into his chair.

"Roy, who do you figure Malone depends on?" Jerry asked.

"From what I saw, half and more of the county."

"Someone's got to them. Malone couldn't do it all himself. Who spread the word? It'll be the men who faced up to you the morning Malone filed. Who were they?"

"Matt Unger came close to a draw."

Jerry nodded. "He was a close friend of Jim Malone and we've picked up some of his beef. One of the old-timers around San Alma. He'd be bound to head up something like this."

"What about John Dean?"

"I've been expecting trouble from him for some time. We've left him alone, of course, to keep us clean in this

123

county. But my kind and bankers don't mix. We've hurt his business. So, there's John Dean. Who else?"

Cantro named Lashlee, Sears, Tip Johnson and townsmen he had seen. Jerry made mental notes of each name. Cantro finished and looked toward Dane. "Frank, any I've missed?"

Dane jerked, startled out of his thoughts. He caught Hallie's pitying, speculative look and then, with a frightened glance, shook his head. "I reckon not."

Jerry steepled his fingers. "I think we'll leave Dean alone, at least for now. Take care of the others and he's no trouble."

"He ought to be taught a lesson," Chulo growled.

"Oh, he'll get it. Later. There's Doc Vance. We'd better leave him alone, too. Kill an old goat like that and you kick up too much trouble."

"Sounds like we're getting nowhere," Cantro said.

Jerry pushed himself up. "But we are! I'm beginning to see how this will work. I'm sending some of the boys to Riata. You'll hear of trouble down there. Matt Unger interests me, too."

"What do I do?" Cantro asked.

"Ride a piece with me and Chulo. I'll tell you the first steps we'll take. You can head home, Frank. I'll let you know what I want you to do. Just be ready. And I haven't forgotten that other idea. Keep your daughter ready, too."

Disregarding the ugly pallor on the old man's face, Jerry gave a signal to Chulo. Cantro turned to Hallie. Something in her expression made his black eyes widen. He started to speak but Jerry made an impatient sound at the door.

"I . . . I'll see you later," he said in a low voice. She didn't answer. Only the harsh control of her will kept her from an angry explosion. "It's not what you think, Hallie."

"Isn't it?"

"I tell you—"

"Roy!" Jerry snapped. "Let's ride."

Cantro gave her a long, searching look that silently begged for a chance to explain. Her frozen features rejected the plea. He wheeled about and went out the door with Jerry, Chulo following them.

Frank Dane moved slowly, as though under an immense weight. He met Hallie's glare, read her anguish. She sensed his understanding and her eyes misted.

He walked slowly to the door. "You or Alice," he said heavily. "It doesn't matter who's hurt so long as Hecker . . ." He looked at her. "What do we do?"

She had no answer. He sighed and put on his hat. "You've found out what Roy's really like. So have I. But I've also learned a lot about myself—and I don't like it."

He walked out shaking his head. Then there was only a desolate, final silence.

The next morning, Frank Dane entered his store and walked with slow, heavy tread down the aisle to his office. He closed the door, placed his hat on the rack and sat down at the desk.

Early sun streamed in the window, but Frank was not aware of it. He stared at the big store ledger under the pigeon-holes of the rolltop desk.

A discreet knock brought his head around in a petulant jerk. The clerk entered and asked a question about stock that Frank answered briefly. "I don't want to see anyone for a while. Not even you," he added.

The clerk, puzzled, closed the door and Frank again stared at the ledger. He remembered how Alice had hopefully searched his face this morning for some sign of relenting. He wanted to—badly—but fear, as usual, had stopped him.

He sighed, folded his hands and frowned darkly toward the window, feeling despondency roll in like a wave. He nearly asked himself why he had become mixed up with Jerry Hecker and Roy Cantro, but he knew the answer before the question was formed. Money.

His scowl deepened. At first, business and the making of money had been an anesthetic against the grievous wound of his wife's death. Then he had seen it as a means of building security for Alice when he himself would be gone. Nothing wrong in those motives. But, he admitted, they had long been fulfilled.

Now he was in the habit. He liked to watch his bank balance and property grow and he liked devising new means to make more. He could see the devious path by which he had moved from good motives, to making it a game, to having it become an obsession.

Last night he had fully realized the manner of man he dealt with, the mire into which he had walked with his eyes wide open. He bleakly considered it all now.

First, Cantro's suit, unwelcomed by Alice, that Frank had been forced to forward. Then Breck Malone had returned. He shuddered when he thought of the panic that had engulfed him when Breck had filed for sheriff. Frank saw exposure and disgrace just beyond election day and fear of this had taken him to that unholy parley last night at Hallie Yates'.

He had hoped they would find some way out. Instead, he faced a worse dilemma. If Hecker decided upon it, Frank must help ruin his daughter's reputation. Just as bad, he had been part of a conference that planned the death of the man Alice loved.

He looked at the heavy, steel safe in the far corner, its knob and handle catching the sun. A new light came into Frank's eyes. He pulled himself from the chair and walked to the safe, grunting as he bent his knees and worked the combination. In a moment, the door swung open and he took a tin box from the shelf.

He stood up—box under his arm—one hand absently stroking it as he looked out the window. His jaw firmed and he picked up his hat and strode out to the street. He looked toward the Cattleman Saloon and saw two familiar saddled horses. He glanced toward the sheriff's office and something like sardonic, pleased laughter showed in his eyes. Then he crossed the street with a purposeful stride.

He halted just within the batwings. Jerry Hecker and Chulo sat at a table in a far corner. Jerry looked up and his flecked eyes swept over Frank, resting briefly on the tin box which Frank placed on the table.

"Sit down, Frank. What's on your mind?"

"I can do this standing up. I figure my cut of what I sold for you over the years is around seven thousand dollars. Is that right?"

Jerry laughed, puzzled. "How do I know? I could figure it, I suppose. But why should I?"

"Seven will more'n cover it."

"Frank, I've got other things on my mind."

Dane opened the box and counted bills until a stack stood before Jerry's small hands. He placed the remainder in the box and closed it with an air of satisfaction.

"There it is."

Jerry's eyes were level and cold. "What are you telling me?"

"I've paid you back every wrong penny. So I'm through. You can jail me if you want to, but damned if you can harm Alice."

"Suppose I say I don't intend to?"

"I'm still through." Frank took a deep breath. "I reckon you'll do something to me for this."

"You've made up your mind. Why should I stop you?"

Frank blinked in surprise. Then his eyes sharpened. Jerry's expression was smooth and unreadable. Frank shifted his weight from one foot to the other. "Well, there it is. You understand it was Alice."

"I understand. Now get out."

Frank turned on his heel and strode out the door. Chulo looked at the swinging batwings, his jaw hanging. "Now what do you make of that!"

Jerry counted the money. "Why, the man quit."

126

"But he can't!"

"He has, Chulo." Jerry looked musingly toward the bat-wings. "Isn't this one of the nights Frank stays to lock up the store?"

"Sure, but—"

"And Breck Malone's probably out at Circle M. He and Frank have been quarreling. Everyone knows it."

Chulo frowned. "But his crew will be with him."

"Now do you think Judge Tracy would let them act as witnesses for Malone? They're his friends—and prejudiced."

"Where you heading?"

"I keep worrying about how late Frank Dane works. Suppose he never gets home and it looks like two or three riders caught him on a dark street?"

Chulo grinned. "Supposing?"

Jerry picked up the money. "Why, find out, Chulo. Cantro and me will be right here tonight if you happen to run onto a murder and need the sheriff."

Chapter XVII

BRECK, LASHLEE and Sears left Circle M by prearranged plan, heading southward toward Riata. The first night they camped many miles from San Alma and rolled wearily into their blankets about the time Jerry Hecker angrily paced the room of Hallie Yates' cottage.

The three were up at the crack of dawn and headed southward. They rode at an easy pace so it was mid-morning before they entered the passes through the Granadas. There were ranches, a mine or two and even a lumbering operation that supplied building materials for both San Alma and Riata. A cluster of houses around a store and saloon boasted the name of Granada and serviced these far-flung mountain enterprises.

In the log saloon high in the mountains, Breck did his first campaigning to an audience of, perhaps, ten men. Lashlee introduced Breck as the next sheriff of San Alma. There was a long moment of skeptical silence. Then a puncher at the far end of the bar asked disbelievingly, "Has Cantro quit?"

"No, but he'll have to if you vote for me," Breck answered.

"Are you a friend of Jerry Hecker's?"

"Far from it."

"Then you ain't got a chance. It'll take more'n votes to beat Cantro. It takes outlaw backing. You ain't got it, you won't get a law badge. You'll get a grave."

"That's where you're wrong. If there's anything Hecker's afraid of, it's an honest contest and honest votes."

For fifteen minutes Breck held the small group in rapt attention. He told them of the organization of hardworking, honest men behind him and their hopes of throwing off the outlaw rule if they could only win this election. Then he waited, half afraid of what they might say. These men were typical of all who would listen to him and he felt their reaction would be an indication of what might happen election day.

The bartender broke the silence. "You talk good, Malone, but how do we know you can back it? If you ain't fast with a gun, you'll be dead. I know what'd happen then to anyone who voted for you."

128

Lashlee laughed and spoke of the wild, lawless towns along the border, of rustlers and outlaw bands. His listeners began to study Breck with a new respect as Lashlee spoke of the ranches for which Breck had worked and his participation in the constant war with renegades who raided and killed on both sides of the Mexican line.

There was another silence when Lashlee finished. The puncher at the end of the bar eyed Breck from boots to Stetson. He searched Breck's angular face, then looked at the holstered Colt.

"Well, now," he said at last, "maybe you're the one we've been hoping would ride along."

Another spoke up. "I knew Jim Malone. A good man and a hard fighter. Hecker beat him only because he was old and tired."

"And discouraged," Breck put in. "He fought alone and nobody'd back him."

"Too scared." The man grinned at Breck. "But I don't reckon you'll get discouraged. Sure sounds like you can fight, too. You can count on a vote from me—or anything else I can do to help."

Breck's face lighted as he heard murmurs of assent from the others. New confidence flooded into him as he saw confirmation of Matt's statement that these people only needed someone to rally behind.

His smile widened when the bartender leaned across the counter and spoke gravely to his friends. "Malone here can't talk to everyone in the mountains. I figure each of us should spread the word that we can elect a sheriff who don't wear an outlaw brand. How about it?"

The puncher's hand slapped down on the bar. "I'm talking high, wide and handsome to everyone I meet. Malone, you can sure count on us."

Breck's reception at Granada proved an accurate forecast of the whole trip. They rode out of the mountains and made a wide swing around the ranches, towns and hamlets in this part of the county. They talked at every opportunity—sometimes to a rancher and his riders, again to larger groups in saloons. In Riata, Lashlee arranged for a meeting in the schoolhouse and Breck was amazed at the number of people who gathered. He was frightened and awkward at first. But within a matter of minutes, he sensed that all these people gave their confidence to him, hung hopefully on every word.

Riata was the end of their swing in the southern part of the county. Lashlee and Sears left him here, but he did not start back to Circle M alone. Despite his protests, four men from Riata rode with him.

Breck rode back over the Granadas with mounting elation. He was eager to find out what had happened around San Alma and even more eager now to visit areas west of the valley and north over the Thunders. He felt that he would surely see the end of outlaw rule after election day. There would probably be gunsmoke afterwards, for Hecker would not be defeated by ballots alone. But once that was over, San Alma would know peace and security.

Breck and the four men rode into the Circle M yard ten days after he started the tour. As he came in the gate, he saw Tip and Doc Vance step off the porch of the ranch house. At the same moment, Chuck and Lew appeared in the wide barn door, hands close to their holsters.

Breck waved and spurred his horse, the four riders galloping after him. Tip and Doc were near the corral gate when Breck reined in and swung out of saddle. He faced them with a wide grin. "Count the whole Riata country for us, Doc. Glad you happened to be here. Saves me a ride into town."

"I've been out here every day for more'n a week," Doc said. "So's Matt."

Breck's smile faded as he realized Doc's face was grave. Tip's leathery face was just as stern.

"Something's happened," Breck said.

Doc's eyes flicked to the four strangers. "Come to the house. I'll tell you about it."

Worried, Breck glanced at Tip and indicated the riders. "Rustle up food and bunks for these boys. They'll rest a spell before they head back to Riata."

He turned to Doc and the two of them walked to the porch. The old man looked hard at Breck. "You've heard no news from here?"

"Too much on the move, Doc. What brought you and Matt out here all the time?"

"We wanted to see you before Roy Cantro did. He's looking for you. He's been out here twice."

"Have I disturbed the peace again?"

Doc didn't smile. "Frank Dane was shot two nights after you left."

"Frank! Who did it?"

"No one knows. He was coming home from the store late. He had just turned the corner near his home when two or three riders shot him down. Folks heard the shot and run out, saw the killers ride off but couldn't make out who they were in the dark."

Breck's eyes filled with consternation. "Doc, I've got to get

130

to San Alma. Alice needs me—and I've been riding around the country!"

He whipped about, but Doc's knobby, powerful hand grabbed his arm and swung him back. "Hold up, Breck. It's been hard on Alice, right enough, but she's standing up under it. There's something more you got to know."

"What?"

"Word spread you and Frank quarreled over Alice. Some folks—Cantro among 'em—think you shot him."

"Me! But I wasn't anywhere near. Why should I want to shoot him!"

"I know you didn't. But Cantro's building the thing up and you can bet Hecker's behind it. He come riding out here and you were gone. Matt and me swore you'd left long before the killing, but Cantro says he thinks you circled back, waited for Frank and got him. He'd sure like to jail you for murder. No chance of you being sheriff then."

Breck beat his fist into his palm and looked worriedly toward the corral, where the four Riata men unsaddled their horses. Tip stood by the corral gate. Breck swung back to Doc. "I'm riding into town."

"How will you keep from jail—or a bullet?"

"I'll keep out of jail. As for the bullet, I'll take the chance. Alice needs me, Doc."

Breck ran to the corral. He ordered Tip and the crew to saddle up and asked his four friends to ride with him to San Alma. "I'm going to need you one way or another."

Tip saddled Doc's horse and the cavalcade, Breck in the lead, raced out of the yard in a cloud of dust, taking the road to San Alma.

The miles sped by and soon the town was before them. Breck loosened his gun in its holster. He cut sharply away from the main road, heading in a beeline for the Dane house. They raced down the quiet street and came to a dust-raising, sliding halt before the dwelling.

Breck vaulted from the saddle. "I'll be out as soon as I can. Then we'll tend to some other business."

He had taken no more than a few lunging strides up the walk when the door was flung open and Alice swept out onto the porch. She was dressed in black, a graceful but tragic figure. Breck bounded up the steps.

Her face was drawn and pale, her eyes red-rimmed. She looked at him as though she could not quite believe his presence and then, with a sobbing cry, threw herself into his arms.

"Breck, I've wanted you so!"

"I'm here now." He held her close. Her body shook with

131

sobs as his voice soothed and comforted. "It will be all right. You won't be alone any more."

He gently led her into the house.

The funeral had been almost a week ago, but the aura of sadness and death still clung to the big front room. The blinds were drawn almost to the bottom of the windows so that the room looked ghostly.

Breck led Alice to the sofa. She fought down her sobs, swallowed with difficulty and then looked at him with misty eyes. He held her hands and spoke gently.

"Can you tell me? I've been away. I came in as soon as Doc Vance told me."

"Roy said you were running. I knew it wasn't so."

"Can you talk about it?" he gently insisted.

Alice held his hands tightly as she talked in a low voice, sometimes quivering and faltering. Breck realized that she knew very little about the killing. She confirmed Doc's story that Frank had been met by some riders. The sound of the shot had brought people out of their houses, but they had merely glimpsed the dark figures of the fleeing men.

"Some said two, some three," Alice said. "It was dark and everyone was confused. Dad was—shot through the chest. They brought him home and sent for the doctor. He wasn't —dead yet."

She closed her eyes for a moment and then continued. "I did what I could. He started tossing his head and mumbling. It was something about Jerry Hecker and that he couldn't quit. I couldn't understand it. Then Doc Vance came."

She looked down at the floor, speaking through set teeth. "Father was conscious for a minute or two before he died. He told me something that makes a change, a horrible change."

Her lips trembled. "He asked Doc to leave. Then he told me—"

She suddenly jerked her hands away and buried her face in them. Breck gently touched her shoulder. "Please. Tell me."

"He worked with Jerry Hecker. He said he had done a wrong and evil thing. He asked me to forgive him. He assured me he had quit. Then he was—gone."

She looked at him, eyes streaming. "Breck, I don't know what to say or what to do. I don't know what you'll think—"

"There's nothing for you to do or say. Frank tried to make it right at the end. Hecker and Cantro both held this over him. That's why he was forced to fight me."

She searched his face. "You knew about this?"

"Not all of it."

132

"Breck—we can't be married now. I'm his daughter and he was part of Jerry Hecker's gang. I'll never live it down and you won't—"

He placed his hand gently over her lips, then cupped her face in his hands and looked deep in her eyes.

"Sweetheart, listen to me! I want to marry you. Maybe Frank made a mistake, but he straightened it out. Maybe that was why he was killed. Anyhow, few know about it and they won't talk. They liked Frank too much to harm his memory. You and me are going to get married just as soon as we decently can."

"But—"

"It's made no change in our plans. Now what has Cantro done?"

She shook her head. "He was here. That night. He swore he'd find who killed father. He said he had an idea who did it, but he wouldn't talk about it. He was at the funeral, but I haven't seen him since. Somehow, I didn't want to. I sent word to everyone I wanted to be alone. I don't know what Roy's done."

Breck stood up. "I'll find out."

Alarm instantly showed in her face. "Breck! Should you? He's still furious with you about me."

"I know. But I have to see him." He spoke flatly. "He's saying *I* could have killed Frank and he's spread the suspicion."

"Oh, Breck! No!"

"He knows if he can jail me, I have no chance in the election. I have witnesses who can testify I was miles and miles away. Cantro has to know this."

"Yes, but . . . he might shoot before you can talk."

"He'll have to find a good excuse first. So he'll listen." He held her close again. "I have to see him. From now on, you're going to let me make the decisions and trust me."

"I do! But I'm frightened."

"Don't be. I can take care of myself."

He kissed her again and turned to the door. She stood at the top of the porch steps as he swung into the saddle and reined away. He flung up his arm in a reassuring gesture and spurred down the street, Doc Vance, Tip and the others following.

They turned the corner. The courthouse stood a scant block away. Out of sight of the Dane house now, Breck drew rein and the others crowded in close. He pulled his Colt from the holster, checked the loads and dropped it back into leather again.

"We're riding to the sheriff's office," he said grimly. "Be-

133

yond the courthouse, spread out behind me and be ready for a fast draw. Make no move until I do."

"Do you figure Hecker's bunch will back Cantro?" Tip asked.

"They might if they're around, but it would be the worse thing Hecker could do right now. I figure he'll leave the play to Cantro."

Breck looked at Doc Vance. "When we round the courthouse, you pull in."

Doc drew himself up. "Now if you think I'm going to miss a fight—"

"You are, Doc. If one of us gets hurt, we want you around to help."

Their eyes locked and then Doc angrily lifted the reins. "All right. But there's times I wish I wasn't a sawbones. Like now!"

Breck smiled faintly and touched spurs to his horse. They rode into the courthouse square and slowly circled the aloof building. The business street lay before them.

Their appearance caused a flurry of excitement along the street. As though by magic, everyone vanished into stores. The men rode steadily toward the sheriff's office, hands close to their guns.

Breck spoke over his shoulder, without taking his eyes from the empty street. "Did Doc Vance drop out?"

"Turned off at the courthouse," Tip answered, "and headed down the alley to our right."

Breck nodded and silence fell on the cavalcade. They drew near the sheriff's office and Breck's eyes went to the empty hitchrack before the Cattleman. Hecker's bunch, at least, would not take a hand in the game.

The batwings of the saloon parted and Cantro stood framed. He stared at Breck and the men behind him, who had now spread out in a crescent extending from one walk to the other. Cantro stepped out on the porch. He snugged his holster to his leg, pulled at his hat brim and then stepped into the street. Breck watched the lawman advance steadily toward him and gave the man credit for cold nerve.

Breck held the reins high, both hands in sight, not wanting to give Cantro the faintest excuse for gunplay. He shrewdly judged the narrowing distance between them and just before he knew Cantro would challenge, Breck lifted his right hand and reined in. His voice carried clearly.

"I hear some think I killed Frank Dane."

Cantro, caught off balance by the sudden maneuver, halted, slightly crouched, hand close to his gun. "Plenty do, Malone."

134

"I can prove I wasn't near San Alma that night."

Cantro's smile was thin and harsh. "Can you?"

Breck indicated the four men from Riata. "I have witnesses right here and there are witnesses in Granada—at least ten of them. I can get the whole town of Riata to prove where I was."

"And where was that?" Cantro asked, sarcasm thick in his voice.

"At the schoolhouse, asking them to elect me sheriff." Cantro's face flushed as Breck's voice grew harsh. "I can prove I didn't kill Frank. You knew from the beginning I didn't."

"Are you saying—"

"I intend to find the killer. That's something you should have done, Cantro. But you don't dare."

The sheriff's face turned dark. "I arrest—"

"Better not, Cantro," Breck cut in. "You'd like me in jail, or under your gun. The whole town knows it and so will the county. It won't work."

Cantro glared at him and his black eyes swung to the grim men behind him. Breck spoke before he could answer. "I'll find your killer for you. I'll make a bet here and now it'll be one of Jerry Hecker's bunch, if not Jerry himself. That's why you haven't made an arrest."

Breck leaned over the saddlehorn, eyes locked with the lawman's. "Do one of two things, Cantro. Be the lawman you were in Tres Cruces. Or tell your friends their days in San Alma are numbered—yours with them."

Cantro's face flamed high and his hand dropped to his gun. Then he froze. The men behind Breck had disobeyed his orders. Cantro stared into the black muzzles of seven Colts and then he realized that from the nearby stores men stood with rifles in their hands, the muzzles lowered but ready to snap up and line on him.

Cantro remained frozen, hand taloned over his gun, black eyes moving. Slowly, his hand dropped. He glared at Breck and his lips moved soundlessly.

Then he turned on his heel and stalked away, back stiff and uncompromising.

Chapter XVIII

BRECK KNEW that Hecker's and Cantro's scheme to blame him for the death of Frank Dane had backfired. The sheriff dared not make any arrest, nor could he spread suspicion any longer. So, in a sense, Breck had won.

Still, when he rode back to Circle M late that afternoon, he was worried about Alice. He had returned to her house after the encounter with Cantro and insisted that she marry him as soon as the circuit-riding preacher came to San Alma. She had refused, again saying that her father's dealings with the outlaws had placed a stigma upon her.

This had no basis in fact, as Breck tried to show her. But she was adamant and Breck saw that no logic could affect her present emotionally shocked state. He had finally left her, saying that they would talk this over later and that he would keep in constant touch with her.

He took courage in the knowledge that the showdown with Cantro had shown the sheriff he had no backing in the town. Cantro was bound to tell Jerry Hecker, who would immediately know the strength of the forces against him. Breck knew that Hecker would move fast and strike hard. The problem was to know when and how.

The four men from Riata left for the south the next morning. The day passed with no word from town. There was something ominous in this false peace. Breck busied himself with ranch chores and records preparatory to making an electioneering swing north beyond the Thunders. He decided to ride into San Alma the next day to see if Alice had recovered her emotional balance.

At the corral the following morning, after he had laid out the work for the day, he told Tip of his intentions. The foreman stopped short, leathery face tight. "Riding in alone?"

"Of course. There's work here for you boys."

"Chuck and Lew can handle it. Me, I'll side you."

"No need for it, Tip. What kind of sheriff needs a gun guard even before he wears the badge?"

Tip scratched his head and turned. His face suddenly went blank and then tightened.

"Visitors! And look who it is!"

Breck wheeled around. Jerry Hecker, sitting easily in

the saddle, rode through the yard gate. Just behind him, Chulo Wyeth's powerful figure swayed to the movement of his horse.

Tip spoke urgently. "Lew! Chuck! Get set for trouble."

The four men moved out of the corral, Breck in the lead. As he advanced to meet the riders, hand close to his gun, he sensed Tip and the men spreading out behind him. Jerry Hecker lifted both hands high and, a moment later, Chulo reluctantly lifted his. They came on at the same easy pace.

Jerry stopped his horse a few yards away and Chulo drew up beside him. The dapper outlaw's face was grave as he looked down at Breck. "Morning, Malone."

"What do you want?"

Jerry made a slight move of his lifted arms. "First, to get these hands down, if you're agreeable. Then talk." He saw Breck's sharp glance cut beyond him. "There's just me and Chulo, if that worries you."

"We've got nothing to talk about," Breck said.

"Malone, we've got a hell of a lot to talk about." Jerry smiled then, cockily assured. "And no trouble while we're here. I'm going to hand over my gun and so will Chulo."

He slowly lowered his arms. Breck heard a slight sound as Tip and his men drew their guns. Chulo's thick lips worked angrily, but he held his hands very high. Very slowly, Jerry moved his coat aside, lifted his gun and dropped it at Breck's feet. "Chulo," he said shortly. In another moment the gunman's Colt lay in the dust.

Jerry folded his hands on the saddlehorn. "Peaceful pow-wow."

Breck considered him a moment. "A waste of time, Jerry, but I'll listen."

"Just you and me?"

Breck spoke over his shoulder. "Tip, watch Chulo and keep him right up there in the saddle. Jerry, you can dismount."

"That's real neighborly."

Jerry swung out of the saddle and Breck motioned toward the house. Jerry walked toward it, Breck several steps behind him. They came to the porch.

"This will do," Breck said.

Jerry sat down on the steps. He removed his hat and used a fine white handkerchief to wipe faint dust stains from his forehead. Breck watched him, concealing his respect for the outlaw's courage and bold assurance.

"Last time I was here, I offered a deal," Jerry said. "No need to tell me you've turned it down."

"Then what else is to be said?"

"Why, something in its place."

"Don't you ever quit trying?"

"No more than you. We can meet head on, Malone, as things line out. If that's the way you want it, I won't argue. But a man's a fool not to find an easy way to do something. Depends on you."

"A sellout of my friends?"

"You bristle with honesty like a damn porcupine!" Jerry said wryly. "Let's say this idea is straight from the shoulder. You don't have to do anything for me and my bunch. Want to hear it?"

"No point, but I give you credit for trying and you've come this far."

"I figured you this way," Jerry nodded. "I'm going to talk money and nothing else—no strings, nothing you have to do except say yes or no. I buy Circle M."

He named a price that was more than double the worth of the spread. Breck was staggered by the amount and the firm, no-haggling tone with which Jerry set it. The outlaw watched him closely.

"You'll never come anywhere near that price, Malone. It's like paying you now for ten years of work in building up the place."

"That's right. But you've overreached. You're talking nothing but money, like you said. But there's other things or you wouldn't be willing to pay that price."

Jerry chuckled. "But they don't concern you. I'm handing you ten years of the future without the hard work. Think what that can do for you. Think what it will mean when you marry Alice Dane. Speaking of that, I figured on a wedding present if we get together on this. A sort of bonus."

"And I just sell the ranch?"

Jerry delicately touched his mustache with his fingertip. "Oh, the deal will provide that you're not to ranch or live anywhere in San Alma County. You'll vacate this place and leave the county within a week."

Breck smiled crookedly. "Now the real deal comes out. If I leave, I can't run for sheriff. Cantro wins by default."

"Of course!"

"So I'm selling you a law badge besides a ranch. That's why you'll pay so much."

"It's worth it to me." Jerry placed his elbows on the steps behind him and leaned back. "You know what I have here, Malone. It's the one safe place in the whole country for me and my boys. The law works for me instead of against me, and you can figure how long it took me to work that out. I want to keep it. You can tear it down. Point is, what's that do for you—except gamble your life against me or my gun-hawks. Say you win. You'll still have ten years of work and worry to make Circle M worth what I've just offered."

Jerry's face grew stern. "There's the deal. This time I'm not going to wait for your answer. I ride out of here knowing one way or the other. It's here and now, or not at all."

"If I don't accept?"

"Lots of things can happen. You and me are enemies for sure then, and I don't fool around. But you're not the only one mixed up in this. You have friends and you could have a great deal to do with their health. I know they're scattered —some in Riata, some here in San Alma and in other places. It won't matter much. I can reach them all."

He stood up. "But let's get back to you. Circle M could get as much trouble as the rest. And so could you."

Breck's face was stone-hard. "Threats again."

"And straight out. The time's passed when I'll walk easy around you. Take my offer. Marry Alice Dane and live rich as hell somewhere else. Turn it down and you'll see every-thing destroyed—Circle M, your friends, everything. And then you'll die yourself. There it is, flat out. What's your answer?"

"No!"

Jerry's lips flattened. "I'm sorry to hear that, Malone. In a way, I understand. You're sticking by your friends like I stick by my boys."

"Then why did you bother?"

Jerry shrugged. "I play out every string."

He turned away, but suddenly wheeled back to face Breck. "Malone, figure what you're doing to yourself, and your friends. Is it worth it? This is your last chance to change your mind. How about it?"

"You waste your breath. No."

Jerry studied him a long moment and then, expressionless, turned on his heel and walked toward the corral. Breck fell in behind him.

When they approached the corral, Chulo Wyeth moved to meet Jerry, an unspoken question in his eyes.

Jerry grunted, "We ride."

Breck indicated the two guns lying on the ground. "Tip, unload 'em and give 'em back."

Tip ejected the shells and handed the empty guns to Jerry and Chulo. The outlaws holstered them and mounted their horses. Jerry folded his hands on the saddlehorn, disregarding Chulo's impatient movements.

"Malone, I've wished a lot of times you could be on my side of the fence."

"What's wrong with my side?"

"What kind of talk is that? You mean jail or a hangnoose. Not a chance." He sighed and lifted the reins. "Had things worked out, I wonder how good a team we would've made."

"Who knows?"

"And we'll never know. Just remember, whatever happens now, the choice was yours." He lifted his hand in a grave salute. "See you in hell, Malone."

He reined around and set the spurs. The horse bolted toward the yard gate. Chulo, with a curse, rolled his own spurs and raced after Jerry. They were gone in a billowing cloud of dust.

Tip looked sharply at Breck. "What's this mean?"

"Just what Hecker said—hell. Tip, ride to Running W. Tell them to watch for raid and rustling, day or night. Chuck, head out to Matt Unger. Lew, check every gun and rifle we've got. See that they're loaded and check the ammunition."

Tip cut in. "And what will you be doing?"

"Riding to San Alma. Hit saddle, Tip. No time to waste."

Despite Tip's protests, Breck rode alone to San Alma. He first called on John Dean and told the banker that Jerry Hecker had made the final challenge and that war with the outlaws was now in the open.

Dean sighed and sank back in his desk chair. "I had hoped Hecker wouldn't go this far. But we have to face it, all of us." He smiled without humor. "He's doing us one favor, though. We'll soon know who will stand up to him and who won't."

"I've sent warning to Matt."

"The right move, Breck. He'll get word to Riata. I'll get the news to our friends here in town."

"Is there any way we can hit Hecker first?"

"That hideout of his is a regular fort. We tried it once before and they knocked us off like sitting ducks. We just have to wait until we can catch him out in the open."

Breck sighed and rose. "Gives him all the advantage."

"For a while. Head for the ranch and hole up. I have an idea Jerry will give you most of his attention."

Breck rode to Doc Vance's office. There was no sign of the sheriff and Breck wondered if Cantro had already been called into a war powwow with Hecker. Breck was with the old doctor for some time. They left the office together and went directly to the Dane home.

Alice looked at them in surprise when she answered their knock. Breck kissed her and spoke gravely. "I want you to pack up and come out to Circle M. Right away."

"I can't Breck. People would talk!"

"But you have to." Breck told her of Jerry's ultimatum, of the savage gunplay that might break out at any moment. She listened with increasing fright.

"Jerry knows how much you mean to me," Breck finished, "and he's a man who'll stop at nothing. He might figure that he could make me back down if he had you in his hideout. No matter what, I wouldn't let anything happen to you."

Her face was pale. "But, Breck, would Roy let him do anything like that?"

Doc Vance cut in. "You figure he's in love with you?"

"What else can I think?"

"Think of your father's money. That's what Cantro loves."

Doc Vance told her, then, of Hallie Yates. Alice listened, aghast. When Doc finished, she turned to Breck. "I'll go with you. I hope I never see him again."

"The outlaws may hit us," Breck warned, "but, even so, it's better for you there than alone here."

"People will understand," Doc assured her. "Besides, if you're willing, I'll bring the circuit rider as soon as he comes to San Alma. I know it's what Breck wants."

"More than anything else!" Breck said.

She looked at him a long moment, her eyes growing deeper and lovelier. "Breck, so do I!"

Doc Vance cleared his throat gruffly. "Then git packed. Time enough for that later."

Alice rode to Circle M, followed at nightfall by a gray-haired widow whom Doc Vance used as a practical nurse. She would act as housekeeper and chaperone. Breck breathed easier. He could imagine Cantro's rage when he learned the news, but the battle lines were already clearly drawn. Hallie would be thankful and Breck hoped that now she and Cantro might find a new understanding. Tip and the crew were delighted and practically ecstatic after the first supper cooked by the two women.

"Sure beats man cooking," Tip confided to Breck. "With food like that, you could get hands to work for nothing."

Breck braced himself for trouble, knowing that Cantro would urge Hecker to swift action. Unger dropped by to say he had sent warning south and to report that things were unnaturally quiet in San Alma.

"But I don't like it. You can depend on it. Hell is brewing."

The tense peace continued for three days during which Breck and the crew, always armed, stayed close to the ranch and waited for the blow to strike. Then a rider came with news from Matt Unger. The Riata country had been hit by raids and rustlings. This explained the outlaws' absence from

141

San Alma. There would be a meeting that night at Matt's.

After dusk, Breck passed the guards at Matt's and was admitted to the big room. He was surprised to see Wills of the Running W, some other ranchers from the valley and half a dozen men from town besides Dean, Doc Vance and Lashlee.

Lashlee told of the raids in the Riata country. "They hit half a dozen places and hit them hard. Three ranchers are dead and cattle has been run off. In each place they left word this was only a sample of what will happen if Breck's elected sheriff."

"Terror raids," Breck said.

"More'n that, at least so far as I'm concerned. They hit my place but I drove 'em off. They tried bushwhack, but missed. They tried mighty damn hard to get me."

Dean spoke in anger. "Spread fear and kill the key men in a district—that's Jerry Hecker's idea. How are the folks taking it, Lashlee?"

"It's hard to say. Some are fighting mad and are willing to see this thing through. Others are just plain scared. Some say Breck will be killed before this is over and then Hecker won't have any mercy on those who supported him."

"Most of them scaring out?" Unger asked.

"I don't think so. But if Hecker's gang had stayed a little while longer, he could have hurt us damn bad. Lucky he pulled out. At least, we think he did. There hasn't been a sign of renegade or trouble for two or three days."

Breck frowned. "He'll hit someplace else."

Unger paced before the window with the drawn blind. "If we could figure where and be ready for him—" He stopped short, head cocked, listening.

There was a sudden shout from outside and a blast of gunfire. The window behind Matt smashed as lead crashed into the room. Matt jerked as bullets struck him and he fell headlong.

Breck lunged to the table and blew out the lamp. "The outlaws! This is Riata over again!"

Chapter XIX

THE MEN IN THE ROOM moved quickly to Breck's orders. Lashlee and two others raced to the back of the house to drive off attack from that direction. Breck jumped to the broken window, vaulting Unger's body, and snapped shots at the racing shadows of the attackers.

For long moments, there was only the blaze and thunder of gun answering gun and the crash of bullets through windows and doors. Gunsmoke swirled, acrid and thick in the room.

The outlaws made a sweeping circle of the house and were met by bullets that made them veer off. Renegade fire lessened to scattered shots—enough to tell Breck that they tried to pin the defenders down until a second, more deadly attack could be planned.

Now that the thundering roar of guns had stopped, Breck became aware of sounds within the darkened room. He heard a cursing groan near the door and became aware that someone crouched over Matt Unger, just behind him. Doc's voice sounded in an anguished, muffled curse. "Matt's gone. Probably dead before he hit the floor."

A man snarled near the door. "Who'll help me get some of those sneaking killers!"

"Wait!" Breck snapped. "They'd like us to rush right out and be picked off."

"Do we just sit here?" someone demanded.

Dean spoke out of the darkness. "Follow Malone's orders."

Breck called to the back of the house, "Lashlee! Anyone hurt out there?"

"No, but we tallied an outlaw."

The man had caught a bullet in the side. Doc worked on him, hampered because he dared not ask for a light. Matt's body was carried to another room. Breck ghosted from window to window, trying to locate the outlaws, hidden by shadows, and to plan some counterattack.

Lashlee called from the rear of the house. "No sign of 'em back this way, Breck. Figure we run 'em off?"

As though in answer, a rifle bullet thudded into the wall. A man by the window replied, slamming a shot into the shadowy yard. Breck spoke swiftly as the men pressed about

143

him. He ordered two men to remain in the room and answer any more outlaw shots. He led the remainder back to the kitchen.

"The outlaws think just Matt and two or three of his crew are in here. That's why they're trying to hold us down until Jerry can figure how to rush the house and finish the job."

"He'll sure learn a hard lesson if he does," Lashlee growled.

"I don't intend to wait for him," Breck said shortly. "They've pulled off somewhere beyond the yard. If we can get our horses, we could hit them when they try to rush the house."

Dean whistled softly. "Breck, that'll work! Think we can make it?"

"Worth a try, John." Breck spoke to the others. "No sound when we slip out. Get your horses and make no move until I give the order. Is that understood?"

There was a chorus of assent. Breck eased open the kitchen door and listened. A shot sounded from the front of the house and was answered by one of the men in the big main room.

Breck moved out the door and, at a half crouch, crept across the dark yard toward the looming, black shape of the barn. He held his breath, momentarily expecting an alarm, but he had guessed right about the situation.

They reached the barn and Breck, holding the reins of his horse, looked beyond the darkened house, trying to penetrate the shadows that hid the outlaws. He saw a lick of flame as a smashing shot broke the silence. He marked the location of the ambusher.

He gave quick, low orders, then moved out, leading his horse, keeping to the shadow of the barn. It was a bold maneuver, but the advantage gained would be worth the risk. He heard the soft, muffled fall of hoofs as the others followed him.

Finally Breck swung into saddle and waited until the others were clustered about him. Now and then shots from the outlaw outposts—always answered from the house—broke the night. Breck's eyes cast toward the far edge of the yard, every nerve strained in anticipation.

"There!" Dean hissed.

Breck saw the shifting shadows off to his left as horsemen materialized. The outlaws drifted down on the house from what they thought was an unguarded direction. The fire in front of the house picked up, intending to call attention away from the real danger.

As the outlaws moved in closer, Breck could make out individual shadows of riders and horses. He waited long, tense

144

seconds and then, with a flowing move of arm and hand, slid the Colt from the holster.

"Now!" He raked spurs and threw a slug at the outlaws.

In an instant, the yard erupted in flaming battle. Hoofs drummed as Breck led the charge directly at the flank of the renegades. Guns flamed constantly and rolling thunder filled the yard. Beneath it, came the surprised, frightened yell of the renegades, a scattering of shots snapped off in a hurry.

They milled as they tried to turn to meet this smashing charge from an unexpected direction. Breck slammed another shot as he bore down on the twisting mass. A man yelled and he saw a rider topple. A horse reared high—screaming and kicking—and then fell, tangling other riders, adding to the confusion.

Gun flame licked at him and he heard the whine of bullets. Then the heaving mass broke. Riders streaked off, each outlaw seeking his own safety. Breck's gun knocked one out of the saddle and he saw another fall. He heard a bellowing roar that could only be Chulo Wyeth trying to hold and re-form his men.

Breck tried to work his way to the big gunman, hidden by darkness and the uncertain, darting movements of fighting men. With surprising suddenness, the outlaws were gone. The yard was empty and, from a dozen directions, Breck heard the fading roll of hoofs. The battle was over. The outlaws fled to the safety of their fortress hideout.

Breck sharply called back men who wanted to go in useless pursuit. He knew instinctively that this swift, deadly battle had gone far to break the ruthless power of the outlaws. They would not dare to ride openly and roughshod over the county. Their only safe place now was the guarded valley somewhere up in the Thunders.

Lashlee's voice lifted in a triumphant shout. "We got us a live one over here."

Breck rode to a shadowy group of men clustered about a writhing and cursing figure on the ground. Breck dismounted and pushed to the center of the ring. A match flared and he saw the contorted face of Red Hollings. The match snapped out as Lashlee spoke. "Bring a lantern so we can take a good look at him."

One of Matt's hands raced for the barn. Breck gave orders to check the wounded and the dead. Men began to move toward definite tasks now, instead of milling in triumphant excitement. Lights came on in the house and lanterns were brought out into the yard.

Doc Vance pushed through the crowd and Breck asked sharply, "Any more hit in the house, Doc?"

145

"No, but it's hard losing Matt. Wills of Running W is patched up. Anyone out here?"

"We got us an outlaw. I don't know how bad he's hit."

A man came with a lantern and Doc crouched over Red Hollings, then looked up. "Bullet crease in his side and a broken leg."

Lashlee pointed to a dead horse. "He was pinned under it."

"I'll patch him up," Doc said.

"Wait, Doc." Breck looked down at Red. "Who led this raid? Hecker?"

"Why don't you find out?" Red snarled.

"You'll tell me."

"Be damned."

"You will be, Red, unless you talk." Breck met the man's defiant glare. "Matt Unger is dead and it can't be called anything but murder. Another man's wounded."

"Their bad luck." Red grimaced in pain.

"No, yours."

"You're wasting time. Have your sawbones patch me up and then take me to jail."

"Not until you tell us who led this raid and those around Riata. You can tell us how Cantro and Tracy are tied in with your gang. You're going to tell us enough so we can jail every living one of you, if you're not shot first."

Red tried to laugh. "Are you crazy?"

Breck spoke with grim patience. "Read sign, Red, and read it fast. Hecker's desperate and you know it. That's why all those raids down south and this one tonight. Roy Cantro's through as sheriff, come election day, and you can bet we're not going to turn you over to him. You won't get a chance to go to Tracy's court and be released. Matt Unger was murdered. Unless you talk, you'll pay for it."

"You can't prove—"

"We don't have to."

"The hell you don't!"

Breck looked around at the circle of grim men. "There's only renegade law in San Alma, and that means no law at all. I reckon we had better act as a vigilante committee."

John Dean looked troubled, then read something in Breck's face that made him glance swiftly at Red. The outlaw looked from face to face and, in each deadly expression, read a threat to himself, immediate and final.

Breck still faced the men. "No need to present the evidence against Red Hollings. We all saw it. Is he guilty of the murder of Matt Unger?"

They immediately shouted assent. Red Hollings pushed up on an elbow, hardly aware of the stabbing pain of his broken

146

leg. His face paled. "Now wait! You can't prove it was my bullet—"

Breck disregarded him. "Bring a rope and a horse."

Red stared in mounting horror as a man appeared with a coil of rope. Someone led up a horse. Red was placed in the saddle. A noose dropped over his head and the loop tightened. Sheer terror paralyzed his throat as the horse was led under a tree and the rope thrown over a stout limb.

As it tightened, his voice returned in a scream. "No! Wait! You can't do this!"

Breck stepped close. "We can and will—unless you talk."

"Anything! I'll tell. What do you want to know?"

Breck asked the questions and Red—now a quivering mass of fright—answered, fairly babbling in his eagerness to tell all he knew and avoid the hangnoose.

Chulo Wyeth had led this raid on Jerry Hecker's orders. The raids in the Riata district had been led by Hecker himself. Red disclosed that one of the main objectives had been the death of Lashlee, but that had failed.

Breck soon had the story of Hecker's agreement with Cantro. Much of what Red told was already known or guessed at by the grim men who listened. But here was the actual statement of places, times and events. Cantro had looked the other way, lost trails and arrested when he knew that Judge Tracy would release, in return for a share of the outlaw loot.

Red's babbling voice quickly disposed of the judge. "Tracy does as Jerry tells him. If he finds one of us guilty, he gives us a little fine or throws the case out. Either way, the law says we can't be tried for that again. We're safe."

"And how much does Tracy get?" Breck demanded.

"Mostly whiskey—enough to keep him drunk—and what little money he needs." Red looked fearfully around the ring of grim men, then back to Breck. "I've told you now. Are you going to let me go?"

"Hang him!" one of the men yelled angrily.

Breck shook his head. "No, he goes to trial."

"Before Judge Tracy?"

"We're writing to the governor tonight. All of us will sign it. We'll send it by rider to the capitol. Judge Tracy will be removed. We'll hold Red prisoner until a new judge comes to San Alma."

"What about Cantro?" Lashlee asked.

Breck smiled tightly. "Election's three days off. By tomorrow, news of Matt's killing will be everywhere. Hecker's finished and Cantro with him. After election, real law will come to San Alma."

The next day, Breck headed a grim procession into San Alma. The heavily armed horsemen surrounded a buckboard on which Matt Unger's body lay, wrapped in blankets. Word of his killing spread. The silent cavalcade created curiosity and alarm.

By the time Breck came to the town's business section, the sidewalks were lined with townsmen who watched in silent tension. Breck saw mute anger on the faces of many as they looked at the blanket-shrouded body on the buckboard.

He looked toward the Cattleman and saw no horses at its rack, an almost sure sign that the outlaws were not in town. The sheriff's office showed no sign of life. Breck's lips thinned as he turned in at the barber's, who also acted as San Alma's undertaker.

Not long after, he came out with Doc Vance, Lashlee and two others. They remounted and the riders moved with grim determination to the sheriff's office. The door was closed and Cantro did not come out. Breck dismounted, then checked Lashlee and the others as they started to swing out of their saddles.

"No need. I can handle this myself."

Lashlee looked at the silent office. His voice lifted so that anyone within the building could hear him. "All right, Breck. We've had enough killings and outlaws now and we aim to see nothing happens. So we'll wait."

Breck's boots rapped across the planks of the low porch as he approached the door. He opened it and stepped inside.

Cantro stood to one side of his desk. His face held more pallor than usual and his black eyes showed a trace of uncertainty. His voice was not quite steady, though he tried to keep it firm.

"I was about to come out. What's wrong now, Malone?"

Breck closed the door. "I think you know. We brought Matt Unger's body in. He was murdered last night in a raid on his place."

Cantro tried to look surprised, but didn't quite bring it off. "Raid! Murder! I'll see about this!"

He took a step, then halted, noting that Breck had not moved from before the door. Breck spoke softly. "If you're smart, you won't show yourself out there."

Cantro's chin came up defiantly. "Why not?"

"Your renegade friends ran into a hornet's nest last night. We hit 'em hard and drove 'em off. They're on the run or hiding up in the Thunders, and you know it."

"What has this to do with me?"

"Don't act any more, Cantro. We know all about your

148

arrangement with Hecker, and Judge Tracy's, too. Right now word's on the way to the governor. The boys outside don't like your looks this morning. I figure it's best to talk to you in here than risk gunplay out there—and have you to bury."

Cantro stood quite still. His eyes searched Breck's face, still half defiantly, then wavered as he tried to call up anger and scorn. "What kind of crazy talk is this?"

Breck looked at him long and searchingly. "What happened to you? What happened between Tres Cruces and here?"

Cantro flinched and his face darkened. His hand half lifted to his holster and then dropped. Breck had made no move for his own gun, but now there was puzzled pity in his eyes.

The sheriff looked away and his voice choked. "Say your piece and get out."

Breck sighed. "Until I came here, I never heard a bad word against you. You had a reputation equal to the best and I figured you were a man to ride the river with. Instead, you're hardly any kind of man at all. What have you done to Hallie?"

"What do you know about her?"

"Enough. More than enough. How have you treated a woman who would do anything in the world for you?—even let you push her aside when you figured a marriage license would give you a lot of money."

"You're asking for a bullet, Malone."

"One wrong move and those men out there would kill you. You might beat me in a draw, but they've got too many guns. I didn't come to talk about Hallie, or Alice. You know how low you've sunk to throw one over and try to force the other to marry you. It's part of what's happened to you."

Breck shook his head. "Your rep's gone. Once, when you wore a law badge, it meant something. Now it's just a tarnished star. People know it, Cantro. You're a renegade. Come election day, the people of San Alma will let you know what they think of you."

Cantro stood stricken, as though Breck held up a mirror and the reflection he saw was ugly and horrible. Breck read a portion of his thoughts in the frozen lines of the strangely pale face.

He spoke gently. "I keep thinking of the Roy Cantro I used to hear so much about. For his sake, I have some advice. Turn in your badge. Ride out and take Hallie, if she'll go after what you've done to her. But ride out, anyhow.

You've got until election day. After that, you'll be dead or in jail."

Breck stepped outside and closed the door. He walked to the hitchrack and became aware of the curious faces of his friends. Lashlee frowned, impatient. "Well, what's Cantro going to do?"

"The right thing...I hope."

"Him? Not a chance! We ought to pull that law badge off him and—" Lashlee saw the harsh frown on Breck's face. He leaned forward on the saddlehorn, uncomprehending. "Breck, sure as hell you're not believing whatever promises he made?"

"He made no promises." Breck swung into the saddle. "But I think he knows where the trail leads, and he'll ride it. Give him the chance."

Breck swung away from the rack. The men followed him, puzzled, but sensing that something had happened inside the sheriff's office. Whatever it was, they would trust Breck. They left the town as grim and silently as they had entered a short time before.

It was decided that Lashlee should stay at Unger's ranch until election day to keep a close watch on Red Hollings. Breck turned off to Circle M, riding slowly and thoughtfully. He felt the loss of Matt, whose energy and force had sparked the move to throw off outlaw rule. He, like Jim Malone, could never be replaced.

Breck's thoughts turned to Roy Cantro. Again he felt regret. The Roy Cantro of Tres Cruces had long been dead. Breck wondered what Cantro would do now. Word of the outlaw defeat would give the whole county new courage. There could be no doubt now how the voting would go. Cantro must know this. Surely, he would not stay around to force his final degradation.

The real fight was almost over. It would take only the official count of the ballots to put the seal on something that had already been done. Breck's face cleared and his eyes sparkled as he thought of it, realized that the trail to the future was now cleared of most obstacles.

He turned in on the ranch road, elated. He would tell Alice it was over. It was but a matter of days now before the circuit-riding preacher would be here.

Breck approached a tangle of bushes and trees. He would be able to see Circle M beyond them and, in his eagerness, he spurred the horse to a fast trot. The distance lessened and Breck smiled as he thought of the happiness his news would bring Alice.

A horse and rider suddenly pushed into the road, and

halted, facing him. Breck drew rein as he recognized the towering shape of Chulo Wyeth. The big gunman sat unmoving, waiting.

Breck's hand dropped to his holster. Chulo saw the gesture and his thick lips moved in an ugly smile. "That's right. It's showdown, Malone."

"Too bad you didn't catch a bullet last night, Chulo."

"The slug that gets me ain't been made yet." Chulo's muddy eyes grew ugly. "You've been riding high, wide and handsome, Malone. It's time you stopped."

"You figure to do it?"

"I've been wanting to for a long time."

"I didn't know Jerry was scared enough to send someone to do his killing for him."

Chulo chuckled. "Jerry ain't scared. Never will be. He just don't bother with tinhorns. Me, I don't care, so I decided last night to do the job myself. I've been waiting."

The slight flick of his eyes was Breck's only warning.

Chapter XX

CHULO'S HAND BLURRED upward, grasped the handle of the Colt and the weapon whipped out with a glitter of light. Each second seemed magnified to Breck. His own hand whipped to the holster and the heavy gun snapped out of leather. Clearly, he saw the black muzzle of Chulo's gun line down on him. His lips pulled back against his teeth as he braced for the smash of the leaden slug. He felt the pull of muscles as his finger tightened around the trigger of his own gun.

The roar of the two shots sounded as one. Breck saw the flash of flame and smoke from Chulo's gun even as his own weapon bucked against his palm. He felt a searing impact along the inside of his left arm. He saw the jerk of Chulo's shirt just below the pit of the throat.

Chulo's body catapulted backward and to one side, his gun spasmodically flung from his fingers in a glittering arc. He hit the ground and his horse skittishly dance-stepped to one side, tossing its head.

Breck swayed in the saddle from the jarring impact of the bullet. His gun was still leveled, hammer dogged back, a thin wisp of blue smoke spiraling from the muzzle and then vanishing. Stunned surprise held him. Chulo's speed had been dazzling and Breck could not understand why he was still alive.

The shock passed in a matter of seconds. Breck felt the warm blood flow down his arm though numbed nerves as yet signalled no pain. He dismounted and, gun still held ready, walked to Chulo's sprawled body.

Chulo's fingers taloned into the ground and he looked up at Breck, muddy eyes showing dull surprise. The front of his shirt was dark now, the stain rapidly spreading. His thick lips moved in a broken, plaintive whisper.

"No one . . . no one beats me . . . to the draw."

His giant chest arched and his body grew rigid. Then it collapsed and his head rolled to one side.

Breck looked down at the dead man, surprise still with him. His arm began to burn. He holstered his gun, unbuttoned his shirt and painfully slipped his arm out of the sleeve.

The wound was a deep gouge in his flesh, bleeding profusely. The slug had missed the bone and Breck quickly improvised a bandage and struggled back into his shirt again. Had Chulo taken a split second longer in which to place his shot, Breck might easily be dead.

He caught Chulo's horse and worked the gunman's body across the saddle. He lashed Chulo's hands and feet beneath the horse's belly and stood back to get his breath. The animal snorted and tossed its head, but Breck held the reins firmly. He mounted and, leading the other animal, headed toward Circle M.

The moment he rode into the yard, Tip and the crew converged on him. The house door flew open and Alice stood poised, fright in every line of her figure. Breck tossed the reins of the horses to Tip and indicated the body.

"Wrap him in a blanket and load him on the buckboard. We'll take him to town."

He hurried to Alice, turning her back to the house. She threw a frightened look over her shoulder and Breck told her what had happened. She stopped, swung around to face him. "Are you hurt?"

"Nicked, nothing more."

She led him into the house and insisted on dressing the wound, making him pull off the shirt and the blood-soaked kerchief he had wrapped around it. She cleansed and dressed it efficiently and calmly. But when it was over, her lips trembled and she suddenly held him close. "Breck!"

"Say, now! It's nothing."

"I know, but just a little to the right and . . ."

She recovered her composure and Breck went out into the yard. The buckboard waited by the corral, the blanket-wrapped body of the gunman a grim mound just behind the seat. Tip and Lew had saddled their horses.

"No telling who you'll meet in town," Tip said. "Chuck will stay to make sure the little lady's safe."

Breck climbed into the seat of the buckboard and drove toward the gate, Tip and Lew flanking him on either side.

Once again, in mid-afternoon, Breck rode into San Alma carrying a dead man on a buckboard. It seemed to him that Chulo's death had evened the score for Matt and he hoped this might end the time of violence.

Once more people stared curiously and gathered outside the sheriff's office as Breck drew rein. He jumped to the ground as Cantro appeared in the doorway. Breck sensed the change in the man. Cantro stood unmoving, something weary and haggard in his eyes. There was no defiance or

153

anger now as he looked at Breck and the figure on the buck-board with a strange lack of curiosity.

His voice was heavy and leaden. "Another one. Who is it this time?"

"Chulo Wyeth. We had a shoot-out."

Cantro started. His black eyes widened in disbelief and he strode to the buckboard and pulled aside the blanket to look upon the gunman's dead face.

"He was Hecker's man, so give him to Jerry," Breck said.

Defiance touched Cantro's lips. "How can I?"

Breck smiled faintly. "I told you the masquerade's over. Tell Hecker he's come to the end of the trail. That goes for you. The string has just about played out."

Cantro looked steadily at Breck for a long moment. The heaviness returned to his voice. "I'll take care of Chulo. Take him to the undertaker."

He turned and walked into his office. Breck thoughtfully rubbed his jaw, then climbed back on the buckboard. Not long after, he drove out of town, the buckboard rattling, free of its load, Tip and Lew still flanking him.

The afternoon before election day, Doc Vance tooled his buggy through the ranch gate. Breck made the old man wel-come. Alice came out on the porch. Doc Vance turned to Breck, grinning as he jerked a thumb toward Alice. "She gets prettier every day! Ranch life is good for her."

Breck put his arm around Alice's shoulder. "She's agreed to be a rancher's lady once the preacher gets here."

"Any day now," Doc nodded.

"What's the news from town?" Breck asked.

"Mostly election. You're sure to win. Folks already treat Cantro like he's not sheriff anymore."

"I had hoped he'd withdraw," Breck said regretfully.

"No sign of it. He stays in his office most times. Maybe he's working up a mad or maybe he thinks some miracle will change things."

Breck frowned. "Or maybe he figures the Hecker gang will show up tomorrow and scare voters away."

"They won't get far. We have plenty of guns of our own. Cantro loses his star tomorrow, no matter what happens."

"Why does he have to play it out to the bitter end?" Alice demanded.

They could not answer.

Early the next morning, Unger's foreman rode into the yard with his crew, all of them armed. Tip, Chuck and Lew were ready to ride. A bay had been hitched to the ranch buggy and Tip led it up to the house. Alice came out.

Breck handed her into the buggy. He turned to the horse Lew had led up and swung into saddle.

On the way to town, men from Running W joined them. There was a suppressed air of triumph about them, an assurance they could not quite acknowledge until the ballot count made it official. Breck felt excitement until they sighted the town some distance ahead.

Tip unobtrusively made sure his Colt would slide easily from the holster. Breck caught the small movement and noticed how some of the gaiety left the men. He glanced at Alice in the buggy and saw, in the lift of her chin and the slight narrowing of her eyes, that she had also been touched by the changing mood.

As they came closer, Breck saw a woman sitting a horse at the side of the road. She moved out, coming toward them at a slow pace. Tip said in a low voice, "Hallie Yates. How come she's meeting us?"

Breck shook his head and, with a word to Alice, rode ahead at a swift trot. The woman drew rein to wait for him. When he came closer, Breck was astounded at the change in her.

She was as strikingly beautiful as ever, but there was strain in her face, a painful set to her lips. A faint hint of dark circles showed under her eyes. He swept off his hat as he drew rein. She spoke in a tight, vibrant voice. "I hoped to see you before Roy did."

"Why? Is he looking for trouble?"

She looked beyond him at the approaching cavalcade. "Can we talk? Alone. It's important."

He signalled to Tip. The foreman drew rein and the riders halted, milling. Tip bent to the buggy, saying something to Alice. The group remained beyond earshot, curiously watching.

Breck turned back to Hallie. "You can talk now."

"I'm worried about Roy."

"He's in trouble. I'm sorry, but it's been coming on."

"I thought maybe I could talk to you."

He read the misery and fright in her eyes and he spoke gently. "Can't you talk to him?"

"I've tried. Up to a few days ago, he'd get mad and argue. But now he's withdrawn and I can't reach him. He doesn't hear me at all. He might as well be a million miles away. He's planning something. I can tell it."

"What?"

"I wish I knew! It scares me."

"Maybe he's going to withdraw."

155

"Not Roy. He never backed away from anything in his life. He won't now."

"Then what can I do, Hallie?"

She looked toward the buggy. "You took Alice Dane away from him. I was thankful for it, but now I think it eats at him. You bested him there and you're bound to beat him in the election. That eats him, too. I'm afraid he'll want to fight."

Breck was silent a moment. "I can't run from it, Hallie."

Her fist beat on the saddlehorn. "I know. But maybe you could manage to avoid it. Please! By tonight he will have lost the election. There'll be nothing for him here, nothing at all. We could start new somewhere. Anywhere. We could leave all this behind us and be together, Roy and me. That is, if he's alive."

"Hallie, I'll do what I can. But what happens is up to him, not me."

Some of the hope left her eyes. She lifted the reins. "I guess that's all I can ask."

She rode away slowly, cutting across the fields toward her small and lonely cottage. Breck looked after her a moment and then waved the cavalcade forward. He saw Alice's questioning look. "She's afraid for her man. Afraid of a gun fight."

"I know. So am I."

San Alma was quiet. Now and then a man or woman on the walk would watch Breck and his riders go by. There was more activity in the square. The polls had been set up in a small room in the courthouse and a long line of voters waited their turn to step behind the curtains and mark their ballots. A few called encouragement to Breck when he rode in. Others smiled as though to tell him he could count on their votes.

Breck told Alice to go to her home, promising that she would be with him tonight when the ballot count was announced. Her hands grasped his. "Come with me! I feel there's going to be trouble."

He smiled at her. "Is this the way for the future wife of a sheriff to act?"

"No, I . . . guess not. But be careful."

She drove away and Breck turned to the polling clerk, the group of riders crowding eagerly behind him. He was asked by those in line to go right ahead and vote, but he smilingly refused and took his place to wait his turn.

Doc Vance came out, saw him and hurried over. He indicated the line. "Been going this way since the polls opened. And peaceful, too."

"How long, though? Until the Hecker gang shows up?"

"Not a sign of them—except Jerry Hecker. He's in the Cattleman."

"Alone?"

"And mean as a wounded bear, I hear."

Breck frowned. "He's got something planned, depend on it. Tell the boys to be ready for trouble."

Doc Vance grinned. "Hell, they've been ready for it since dawn this morning."

Breck finally cast his ballot. He came out, remounted his horse and slowly rode around the courthouse, Tip and half a dozen men following him. He passed the bank, closed now for election day. He headed for the Thunder and saw that horses lined its rack. The Cattleman's rack was bare except for a magnificent saddled black that must be Jerry Hecker's. The door of the sheriff's office was open, but Breck did not see the lawman as he rode by.

He pulled in at the Thunder and had walked to the saloon steps when Tip's urgent voice brought him around. "Breck! It's Cantro!"

Breck stepped clear of the foreman and waited as Cantro approached at a steady pace, the pale face looking more gaunt than ever, but the jaw and mouth rock-hard and determined.

Cantro stopped and Breck realized that the law badge on the man's shirt was brightly polished, catching glints of sunlight with each slight movement. There was nothing about Cantro of the man about to start gunplay, but Breck could not quite check the slight taloning spread of his hand below the holster.

Cantro noticed. His black eyes cut around the crowd, then back to Breck. He took a deep breath.

"Malone, you've caused me nothing but trouble. You've stolen my girl, you've blocked me and fought me. Now you're about to take my badge. I've hated your guts and I've sworn that I'd kill you."

"Is this it, Cantro?"

"The other day you said things that I'd let no man say before—and live."

"The truth has to be told, sooner or later."

Cantro's jaw tightened. "That's right. But I'll tell you something. If there'd been one bit of crowing, one bit of spurring in what you said, you'd be dead now. But you didn't like what you had to say to Roy Cantro, the man from Tres Cruces. Is that right?"

Breck frowned, puzzled. "That's right."

"You talked about the star." Cantro touched the glittering

157

badge. "You were right. It was pretty dirty. It's hard for me to say, but I thank you for telling me."

Cantro looked down at the badge. "Pretty now, ain't it? I've polished it, but I've got to clean it—while I still got the right to wear it."

"I don't understand, Cantro."

"You will, Malone. You will."

The crowd parted as Cantro turned and walked steadily across the street. He took a stand a few feet from the walk before the Cattleman. His voice lifted. "Hecker! Jerry Hecker! Coming out, or do I come in for you?"

Breck gasped. He took a lunging stride toward the sheriff, but Tip's iron grip swung him around. The foreman's leathery face held a strange expression.

"Let be. Let him do this. He must."

The batwings of the Cattleman burst open and Jerry Hecker stepped onto the porch. He was as dapper and neat as ever, the bowler hat set at a jaunty angle. But the face beneath it was harsh, tight, set in ugly lines. His coat was open, pushed back to clear the gun in the holster.

He saw Cantro in surprise. "Now what is this, Roy?"

"I'm arresting you for rustling, bank and stage robbery, murder and conspiracy to murder Frank Dane—to say nothing of Matt Unger and Jim Malone. I can also think of bribing a sheriff and a judge so that they stood by while honest folks were ruined."

"Wings and a halo don't fit you, Roy."

"Maybe I'm trying to find the right size," Cantro snapped. "You're under arrest, Hecker. Coming peaceful?"

"Why, Roy, you know better."

There was a flurry in the crowd and suddenly Hallie Yates burst clear. She gave an agonized cry when she saw Cantro facing Hecker. "Roy! Roy!"

His head half turned, and then he realized his mistake. Jerry's hand streaked to his gun. Cantro twisted about, lips pulled against his teeth as he desperately tried to beat the draw. His gun was half out of the holster when Jerry's bullet hit him. Cantro spun around with the jolt of the slug. He fell on his side, then over on his face and lay still. Hallie screamed and rushed to him.

Jerry calmly holstered his gun and looked at the crowd, contempt in his eyes. "Anyone else?"

Breck threw off Tip's restraining arm and stepped clear. Jerry saw him for the first time and his flecked green eyes lighted in diabolical pleasure.

"Malone! Now you're the gent I came to see."

"You knew it had to be, Hecker."

"Why, yes—so I rode in."

"Alone?"

"Seems like you've scared most of my boys off."

"You're a fool," Breck snapped.

"You forget that a man like me always has to win. My boys figure I'm not so good, but they're still a little afraid of me—those that didn't ride off. So I down you or get a bullet in the back. I like it this way."

Breck stood close to Cantro's sprawled figure. Hallie's sobs wrenched at him, but he dared not give her so much as a glance.

Jerry spoke softly. "Too bad you won't wear the badge, Malone. You might've made a good sheriff. But the election will be settled here—with bullets instead of ballots."

He looked away as he spoke. "You see, Malone—"

His play came with blurring speed, in the hope that his easy talk had caught Breck off balance just enough to give him that precious split second.

Breck moved fast, dropping into a crouch, his hand jumping to his gun. His wrist twisted as he brought the muzzle into line. He saw Jerry's gun wink flame and smoke and his own gun thundered.

A giant fist struck Breck in the chest and he sailed backward. His fingers had no strength and the gun jumped out of them. He hit the earth on back and shoulders and then his head slammed back. Lights exploded and there was a whirling, enveloping darkness.

He opened his eyes to lamplight and he could not understand why he was not before the Cattleman facing Jerry Hecker. This was a room and—suddenly something clicked in his mind and he knew that he had been too slow. The outlaw's bullet had caught him.

He tried to sit up, but could only lift his head for a second before it dropped back on the pillow. He felt so weak! Then Alice bent over him, her face concerned but a glad light in her eyes.

"Lie still, Breck. You're all right."

Doc Vance's grizzled face appeared behind her. She stepped aside and the old man bent over him. "So you decided to wake up, huh? Sure took you a long time."

"Where?" Breck whispered, and wondered why his voice was not stronger.

"My home, darling." Alice again bent over him. "You've lost a lot of blood and you must rest." She understood the puzzled question in his eyes. "Hecker is dead. Don't worry now."

"Cantro?"

159

Doc Vance spoke. "Hecker killed him. But, give Cantro credit, he tried to clean up the mess he made. Outlaw rule is over, Breck. You're the new sheriff, but it won't be the gun job we thought it would be."

Alice's hand smoothed Breck's forehead and he smiled weakly up at her. Doc chuckled. "We got your first job lined out for you, Breck. You'll get married. The preacher just rode in, not more'n an hour ago. By tomorrow you'll be strong enough to get hitched."

Breck's gray eyes lighted. His hand sought Alice's, held it. His fingers tightened around hers and he drifted off into contented, healing sleep.